Two Worlds at the Same Time
FULL SPECTRUM IMPROVISATION
for the Theatre and Life

JOYA CORY

Published 2017
by Lucky Dog Productions
1586 27th Avenue
San Francisco, CA 94122

Printed in the United States of America
ISBN: 978-0-692-86426-5

Book design: Debra Murov
Editor: Jennifer Goheen
Photographers:
Michael Astrauskas, Nonie Kimpitak,
Peter Kosho McKenna, Patti Meyer

Library of Congress Control Number: 2017908695
LUCKY DOG THEATRE, San Francisco, CA

Two Worlds at the Same Time
FULL SPECTRUM IMPROVISATION
for the Theatre and Life
Cory, Joya--1. Improvisation (Acting).

For my beloved guys: Richard, Joshua, Maceo and Carmelo.

CONTENTS

CHAPTER TEN:

CHAPTER ELEVEN:

ACKNOWLEDGMENTS

Many thanks to my esteemed colleagues in improvisation without whom no theatre would be made: Owen Walker, Martin Robinson, Cynthia Moore, Olivia Corson, Craig Landry, Yehudit, Van Phillips, Marcia Aquilar, Fritzi Schnell, Gomez, Elena Gardella, Michael Sommers, Katherine Bettis, David Saniako, Grace Walcott, Greg Lejnieks, Karen Hirst, Ron Jones, Fred Curchack, Brian Narelle, Michelle Coxon, Nina Wise, Suzanne Hellmuth, and other performance partners too numerous to name. Thanks to loyal helpers and friends, Patti Meyer, Judith Basler, Rebecca Kutlin, Rachel Buddeberg and Jacqueline Hayward. Deep gratitude for my many inspiring teachers and to the Z Space Artists' Development Lab for years of creative support. Thanks to my supportive and skillful editor, Jennifer Goheen, and editorial consultant, Steven Schwartz, and to creative book designer, Debra Murov. Thanks to my writer son, Josh, for his heartfelt help and encouragement. And to the love of my life, Richard Kamler, whose devotion to the making of art is an ongoing inspiration.

I'm continually inspired by my students' creativity and courage and am hugely grateful for all I've learned collaborating with them to develop FSI. It's so satisfying to watch them find their way in an improvised piece of theatre, see the aliveness in their faces and bodies and hear the power in their voices. I celebrate their perseverance in learning this challenging art form.

Joya and Suzanne, Berkeley Art Museum 1971

INTRODUCTION

*One does not discover new lands without consenting
to lose sight of the shore for a very long time.*

—*André Gide*

It's December and I'm driving across the San Francisco Bay Bridge in heavy traffic and even heavier rain. Cars are speeding by, going too fast for the wet road. There's a painful spasm in my neck and shoulder.

I turn off the news on the radio, not wanting to hear more about the housing crisis and extreme income inequality in San Francisco, where I live. I'm all too familiar with these troubles.

I'm cursing the pain in my aging body and obsessing about all the unwelcome events in the last year: my husband's injuries and illnesses (requiring a lot of caregiving), my frequent migraines and bouts of depression, financial stress, canceled travel plans. And forgetting, as I do, about the good stuff: loving family and friends, two gorgeous grandsons, a nice house to live in and work I love: teaching, directing and performing Full Spectrum Improvisation.

I arrive in Berkeley, sour as Scrooge, and enter the dance studio my colleagues and I rent for improvisation practice. As soon as I'm in the door I see the large, open space, the smooth wooden floor, the high ceilings and light flooding in through the skylights. This is our special place, our sacred playground.

I feel my shoulders release their clutch. I greet and hug my beloved colleagues. We warm up individually (I lie on a mat, stretch and breathe) and together. Sound and movement fill the studio. Then we watch each other perform.

Craig is up first with a solo about his childhood on the Louisiana Bayou. He begins with movement: shaking his hands in front of him, tiptoeing about the space, making gasping, anxious sounds. Then his words come, rich language integrated with quirky movement and gesture. He describes a day when he was eleven years old, at a big family barbecue, and his grandma caught him and his cousin, Claude, hiding out in the sugar cane, masturbating each other. We feel the shame and yet laugh at the image and his droll delivery. He connects this story to his present life as a gay man. I thoroughly enjoy his piece and tell him so.

When it's my turn to get up, I'm the third, come-in-later actor in a trio with my partners, Owen and Martin. The piece starts with the guys doing some kind of bizarre, off-kilter workout routine in what may be a gym or club in some nether world. They lunge and recover, grunt, and run in place to some rhythm heard only by them. Occasionally they fall into one another or one playfully pushes the other down and helps him get up, blurting out a few lines like "Hey buddy, watch it," "Man, look at you!" and "Go-go-go." After about a minute I feel drawn to enter their world, so I saunter in and join Martin in his running in place.

Martin: (keeps moving and without looking at me says) How did you get in here?

Me: (pause) Uh, I came in through the side door.

Owen: That door is supposed to be locked.

Me: (pause) Well, it isn't.

Martin: (to Owen) I thought you'd talked to maintenance about that.

Owen: (Running slow circles around me): Oh, yeah, I talked to them all right.

Me: Well, I'm glad it was open, 'cause the front door was locked.

Martin: (pause) It seems you don't understand, ma'am.

Me: I don't understand?

Martin: This is a private club. Private.

Owen: Yeah, private.

Owen and Martin, nearly simultaneously, stop in their tracks and look at me. I freeze. The atmosphere is charged. My character is scared (because I am a little scared). The movement re-starts, and new patterns emerge. It feels like a story from my life, though I don't remember ever having had any such encounter with two men in a locked athletic club. My character is clearly having trouble keeping up, physically, as I am. (My scene partners are both much younger than I.)

Martin: (to me) You look familiar.

Me: Oh, yeah? Well, maybe we've met. It's possible.

I start to sing softly to myself the old cowboy song "Don't Fence Me In". (I don't question impulses like this.) Martin responds to my singing with interest, asks me how I know that song. Owen looks at me with disapproval, then makes a show of ignoring me.

Martin starts jumping rope using a rope he's grabbed from our prop table, which is set upstage behind the players. Owen's movement becomes more and more bizarre as his legs bend at weird angles. I resort to making peculiar gestures with my arms, inventing my own "workout" routine.

The scene develops and a story emerges about who belongs and who doesn't. There's mention of the fact that I'm a female. In this discussion, my character stands up to the men, explaining that providence has led me to this spot and I have a right to be there. I am a member, or will soon become one. Martin's character (Owen names him Arnold.) and Owen's character apparently have known each other since high school.

It turns out that I may know Arnold's mother; I'm her age and live near her. This worries Arnold.

After doing what they can, short of physical contact, to eject me/her from the place (it's assumed a gym, not stated.) Arnold changes his mind and says, "Maybe it's OK for her to stay." Arnold and Owen (Owen's character and mine are not named.) end up fighting for dominance. I sit on the floor and watch them as they enact a slow-motion fight/dance, flinching when they release expressive grunts and cries. Owen tries to tie up Arnold/Martin with the jump rope. They both get entangled in it.

After fifteen minutes the piece finds a closing with my character languidly stretching while the two guys lie bloodied (not literally) by each other, one panting, one whimpering, on the floor. As the scene ends I'm singing "Don't Fence Me In" again while Arnold weakly joins me.

Craig, our audience, claps. Martin, Owen, and I smile at each other, acknowledging the pleasure in our connection. We sit down. Craig shares what he liked best about the piece. In this case, there's very little he didn't like. If it hadn't worked, he would have told us his thoughts on why that was. We, the actors, agree, we really enjoyed the work, felt we were all "in the groove." We believe the piece to be so watchable that we wish there had been an audience there. Or a videographer. But it's improvisation, never to be repeated.

I feel transformed. I'm alive and excited. Life looks fascinating again. I'm not aware of any pain in my body. The theatre piece that just emerged from our collaboration is not what anyone could have expected. It's a mystery.

So what happened in the scene described above? How did Martin, Owen and I devise a spontaneous theatre piece that we all agree worked as art and as therapeutic play? What about Craig's solo? What made it succeed? What is it that makes an improvisational theatre piece fail (a frequent occurrence)? What do I mean by "fail" or "succeed?"

Briefly, the scene was satisfying because the players were fully committed to the world of the piece and they worked together with a high degree of cooperation and trust. They have practiced the form together on many occasions and are all skilled in the same style of improvisation. They agree that full, emotionally charged physical life is essential to the art form and that the content must feel meaningful to all.

As for the solo it was thoroughly engaging to witnesses because of the quality of the "writing," movement and voice and because of the skillful integration of these elements: form and content. Craig's story, a childhood memory, was triggered by an image that came to him through his initial movement and sound impulses.

There's much more about the sources of improvised material later in this book. When no emotional reality is off limits, the result is the full spectrum of improvisation.

Michelle and Joya, Berkeley Art Museum 1971

WHAT FSI IS AND WHAT IT ISN'T

TWO WORLDS

The true method of knowledge is experiment.

—*William Blake*

he world of improvisation is a vast territory, an open but defined space, in which all manner of things can be discovered: the possibilities of the body, the voice, the imagination, the joy of give and take with others. In short: deep fun. There is often a sense of belonging to two worlds at the same time: the inner world of the psyche and spirit and the outer world of material reality. It is this simultaneous awareness, and the merging of these realities, that I love most about theatre, especially improvisational theatre.

One of the fundamental challenges of improvisation is how to move into this altered state, often called being "in the groove," "in the zone," or "in the flow," at will. This heightened state of concentration is where we have full access to our deepest stories and to the various "characters" that live within us. The state of unfettered imagination, of deep connection with instinct and intuition, wedded to a sense of craft, is a great high, a brief vacation from the material plane. Though it may sound highfalutin to say that improvisation can be a spiritual activity, really most art is, in that artists are seeking transcendence, some kind of transformation. And of course, the roots of theatre are in religious ritual. I'm not very religious, but I likely would be if I didn't have theatre and art in my everyday life. The need for mystery, for ritual and celebration, is met when I enter the world of the creative act.

Many of the principles and exercises in this book address the task of finding "the zone" and the ever-present challenge of what to do when we're not there, when we're plagued by self-doubt, not connected to our self or our partners. Every improviser, indeed, every artist, at all levels of skill, has experienced this painful and

distressing state. You'll find an essay on handling stage fright, with suggestions for performers and anyone else who wants to be more at ease in front of an audience, as well as techniques to help "save" a failing piece on stage.

Our training expands expressiveness by coaxing away barriers that stifle an authentic response to stimuli. The most common block is inhibition caused by the inner critic, so a core part of our training is learning to release from judgment, to trust our intuition.

PERSONAL TRANSFORMATION

Improvisational acting is wonderfully suited as a tool for personal transformation because the instrument in this art form is the self: the body and psyche.

Full Spectrum Improvisation has given me a safe place to be my largest, most vital self. When I find myself feeling emotionally or spiritually disconnected or deadened, I trust that if I am able to go to the studio, preferably (but not necessarily) with other trusted improvisers, our practice will unearth themes, movement, emo-

tions, images and stories that were not previously available to us.

Improvisation is also an effective tool for devising and developing new scripts. I've written five solo pieces and several collectively created pieces using the experimental process I learned as an improviser. After all, improvised language is writing on our feet.

Full Spectrum Improvisation can be fruitfully studied and practiced by performers from beginners to professionals, ideally in conjunction with classes led by a teacher skilled in improvisational theatre or creative movement, acting, and/or drama therapy. This book presents philosophy, techniques and exercises that can be used to create spontaneous theatre worth watching and can also be enjoyed by anyone interested in theories of creativity and/or exploration involving the body, voice and imagination. The principles and exercises described here can be used by non-performers for creative play or to reduce the fear of public speaking. As to the question of Full Spectrum Improvisation as theatre and as a therapeutic alliance: it is both.

WHY IS IT CALLED "FULL SPECTRUM?"

A student in one of my beginning FSI classes said he'd heard that if you had improv skills, you could go anywhere where improvisers spoke the same language and perform with them. I told him that, from my point of view, that was true only in the sense that a bluegrass fiddler could play music with a classical violinist: same instrument, different style, different esthetic. Successful collaboration would depend on the musicians' range of skills. As improvisational theatre is an intensely collaborative activity, all actors in an ensemble must agree on what style they'll perform together.

The word improvisation covers a vast range of creative possibilities: jazz and new music, post-modern dance, short form and long form language-based improv comedy, psychodrama and Playback Theatre. Then there is the physical theatre variety based on movement but including language, sometimes poetic, often abstract. Or storytelling integrated with dance. Over the years, as I've developed my approach, my challenge has been to meld the freedom, musicality, sensuality and visual imagery of physical theatre with aspects of narrative improvisation that are the most resonant for me: felt emotional life, developed relationships and satisfying stories.

Full Spectrum Improvisation has much in common with the structures used by actors doing long-form comedy improv and, at the other end of the stylistic spectrum, dance-based improvisation. The performance pieces are spontaneously created, and the basic assumption of ensemble collaboration, accepting your partners' impulses and building on them—the YES, AND principle—is practiced, though in FSI this principle is adjusted to meet the need for authenticity.

Although many of the pieces that are created in FSI workshops and performances are hilarious (incongruity and surprise, intrinsic to improvisation, are core elements of comedy), there are often pieces that are poignant and poetic. One of the wonders of practicing theatre is that it can provide the needed release of both laughter and tears. If we feel a need to lighten a piece, we can use comedic techniques like exaggeration, word play, repetition and eccentric movement. Finding meaningful content and artful language is more challenging. FSI performances may include broad physical comedy, elegant dance, naturalistic dialogue, direct address storytelling and rants or rhythmic riffs within one piece.

It's called Full Spectrum Improvisation because we embrace the whole range of emotional life, the shadow as well as the light, as is assumed in acting. In this way, FSI differs from comedy improv, which focuses on the lighter side. And, though we work in depth with language, our training is body-based and often includes working with musical accompaniment.

A THERAPEUTIC ALLIANCE

All art, including comedy, should be subversive. This requires taking risks with your idea of yourself, your images of masculinity or femininity, your concept of dignity. We can shift the way we think about ourselves, expanding our ways of being in the world. This is profoundly therapeutic and works as an adjunct to support other forms of psychotherapy.

Psychologist Eberhard Scheiffele writes about this overlap. He explored the altered state of consciousness experienced by actors and improvisers in his scholarly paper "Acting: An Altered State of Consciousness." He quotes G. William Farthing in *The Psychology of Consciousness*:

> Actors (in performance, drama classes, or in psychodrama) routinely enter into an altered state of consciousness (ASC). Acting is seen as altering most of the dimensions of changed subjective experience which characterize ASCs according to Farthing, namely: attention, perception, imagery and fantasy, inner speech, memory, higher-level thought processes, meaning, time experience, emotional feeling and expression, self-control, suggestibility, body image, and sense of personal identity.

In Europe the special contributions of the abstract, the surreal, the irrational and the subconscious have been part of the stage tradition for centuries. From the 1990s onwards, a growing number of European improv groups have been set up specifically to explore the possibilities offered by the use of the abstract in improvised performance, including dance, movement, sound, music, mask work, and so on. These groups are not especially interested in comedy, either as a technique or as an effect, but rather in expanding the improv genre so as to incorporate techniques and approaches that have long been a legitimate part of European theatre.

FSI's aesthetic was developed out of my exposure to the European improv forms described above melded with techniques of American Long Form Improv. I feel deeply connected to and influenced by my training with Jerzy Grotowski's Polish Laboratory Theatre and with Anna Halprin who, though American, is in this experimental tradition of exploring dance, sound, images and the abstract in improvised performance.

ORIGINS OF FSI, PHILOSOPHY AND AESTHETIC

The creation of something new is not accomplished by the intellect but by the play instinct acting from inner necessity.

—*Carl Jung*

I think of Full Spectrum Improvisation as experimental theatre, a term used in the 1970s and 80s when I was coming of age as a performer and teacher. As we know, San Francisco in the late 1960s through to the early 1980s was a hotbed of social and political upheaval, providing fertile ground for intense experimentation in the arts. As a very young performer, I was living in the Haight-Ashbury and earnestly believing that we (myself and my cohort of idealistic hippie activists and artists) were engaged in Changing the World (caps intended), needing to believe that we were doing our bit to make the world better in some way. And, of course, the world did change, is always changing. Just not always for the better.

A friend once said to me, "You have a tragic view of life. Chekhovian." I agree (Jewish, child of a refugee mother and a bipolar father). I'm not a YES, AND type of person, not naturally optimistic. As a child and adolescent, I felt myself as the outsider, felt I didn't belong anywhere, until I discovered dance and, later, theatre. I found, in exploring those art forms, another version of myself, where my rebellious and restless nature could be an asset. My frustration became energy that I could use to create something new and exciting.

It's said that we teach what we need to learn, so I embraced YES, AND and discovered that I could bring everything with me to the world of improvisation. Every feeling and thought, every impulse and idea can feed our creative play.

EARLY DANCE

My first experience of dance training was at age four, taking classes with my Aunt Ethel in Isadora Duncan's lyric dance. We flew around the studio in loose tunics and bare feet, waving long silk scarves. Later, I took ballet and modern and jazz dance. Oh, I loved my dance classes.

In 1969, after years of studying ballet as a child and teenager and having decided that it wasn't for me, I heard about Anna Halprin's Dancer's Workshop. I signed up for classes and loved it. The performance form we were learning had an anarchistic feel and danced along the borders between post-modern dance, theatre, performance art and ritual in a way I had never seen.

In the intensive apprenticeship program, the atmosphere of free investigation and discovery suited my nature and formed my non-doctrinaire attitude toward creative work. Anna Halprin's (she was called Ann at that time) training helped me throw off the shackles of ladylike behavior. I was also fiercely embracing feminist theory at the time and was involved in women's support and political action groups. There were gripping street theatre events like "Take Back The Night," produced by Starhawk, involving hundreds of women. The first solo performance piece I directed, in the early 1980s, The Adventures of Scarlot Harlot, was by Carol Leigh, a working call girl who had studied poetry at graduate level at Brown University.

At the Dancer's Workshop I met Suzanne Hellmuth, the performer with whom I would found, in 1971, Motion: The Women's Performing Collective, a feminist experimental troupe that performed evening-length, improvised, physical theatre pieces. During our Dancer's Workshop apprenticeship program, we performed outside on Anna's wooded Marin dance deck and did urban street theatre around San Francisco. Suzanne created a piece she called "Saint Vitus Dance," which we performed as street theatre around the studio neighborhood. There was lots of drumming, chanting, colorful costumes and wild dancing, which some neighbors interpreted as the behavior of a tribe (there were about sixteen of us) of drug-addled hippies. One of the neighbors called the police, and the tactical squad arrived in full riot gear. A filmmaker who had been shooting at the workshop for days recorded the event. We were interviewed by police, and some were handcuffed, loaded into the squad car, and taken to the station to be booked for disturbing the peace. I found it thrilling and ridiculous that we performers were viewed as a threat to an orderly world. It was my first taste of the power of theatre. When footage of the bust was aired on the news that night, all charges against the dancers were dropped. We created a lot of street theatre pieces in that training, which taught me about the need for commitment and courage in making art.

In 1972, Suzanne and I were joined by performer Nina Wise. We worked as a threesome, with intervals of other women performers joining us, until 1978 when Suzanne dropped out. We spent many hours exploring and experimenting in the studio, sensing for new forms and structures. Nina and I, along with designer Lauren Elder, worked together for several more years, eventually making scripted pieces. MOTION performers also taught workshops in many venues, including the women's section of the San Francisco County Jail. Exciting times, full of learning.

Around 1970, I started taking classes in San Francisco at The Committee, a spinoff of the pioneering Second City improvisational comedy group in Chicago. Their focus was topical and satirical. This was a very different approach to improvisation (from Anna Halprin's), with choices coming from the intellect, concerned with timely political content and a primary commitment to comedy. When I encountered improvisation in these two different forms, dance and theatre, it was a revelation to me. I had not even imagined that I could express myself so freely and powerfully in movement and in language. And it felt absolutely natural. There was a deep level of connectedness with my fellow players that had little to do with the usual rituals of conversation.

During the 1970s and 80s, I trained with Grotowski's teachers who offered summer workshops in Berkeley. Their training was so rigorous and exhausting, both physically and emotionally, that it became very difficult to hold on to habitual inhibitions about revealing feeling. During these workshops self-consciousness dropped away. This was a profound relief for my performer self and for my everyday self in the world.

I also studied with teachers at American Conservatory Theater, Roy Hart Theatre, Joseph Chaikin (Open Theatre), and sundry other acting, improvisation, movement and voice teachers. I found something of value in most approaches. In 1983, I returned to San Francisco State University in the MA program in theatre (I had studied psychology my first two years of college, before deciding on theatre) but stayed only one year, opting instead to accept an Artists in Social Institutions grant from the California State Arts Council, which placed me in an addiction recovery center, teaching classes in improvisational movement to the clients. I taught for ten years at two different alcohol/drug treatment residential centers and found that offering addicts techniques that could alter their psychophysical state without drugs was a valuable part of their recovery. They could learn how to play, relax, and get high while sober, a rare experience for many of the clients. I rarely dealt with the content of these folks' lives. There were therapists on staff for that.

Then I began working as an actor in scripted theatre, all the while studying and practicing a variety of improvisational theatre styles, and studying improvisational dance with John Graham, who imbued his approach with spirituality and mysticism. This fit with a parallel study of Buddhism and meditation at that time. Other early influences include Mary Overlie (Viewpoints) and Bay Area colleagues: Jani Novak, Ruth Zaporah, Terry Sendgraff, The Blake Street Hawkeyes, Lilith Theatre and the Firehouse Theatre.

In the late 1970s–early 80s, I took a series of summer intensives with Keith Johnstone, who came down each year from Canada. He taught Theatre Sports, but he emphasized narrative skills and told us he made up the "Sports" part just to get audiences involved. Meanwhile, I continued regular acting training with Jean Shelton School, John Argue, Abigail van Alyn, Richard Seyd, and others, mostly in the Bay Area, but occasionally I'd travel to New York, Los Angeles, or other locations for training.

In 1984 I stopped performing publicly as an improviser, although I kept practicing and continued directing my troupe. I never stopped teaching it and thinking about it. Although I had (and have) complete faith in improvisation's therapeutic value and its effectiveness as a tool for expanding acting skills, I had become frustrated with its limitations as a performance form: it's lack of reliability and the ever-present risk of creating incoherent or shallow theatre in the service of spontaneity.

I focused on acting in scripted plays and directing and writing solo plays and teaching Solo Performance, in which performers develop written pieces with the help of improvisation and writing technique. This frustration with improvisational performance, which I loved doing, pushed me to develop what I later called Full Spectrum Improvisation, which draws on principles and exercises from physical theatre, dramatic and narrative improvisation, Method Acting, movement Viewpoints, comedy improv, creative play and drama therapy.

I returned to improvised performing with a renewed and clearer sense of its possibilities. It is what Susan Sontag calls "small audience art": intimate, informal, potentially very personal, and very much worth doing. In 1990 I formed Lucky Dog Theatre, a troupe that performs FSI and has since had several different casts.

In Full Spectrum Improvisation, we take a laboratory approach in which failure is accepted as essential to learning. Improvisation as performance can have a high failure rate, so an effective process of recovery is essential.

We train to develop our intuition, a flexible body and voice, acting skills, and the ability to "write on our feet." We practice listening intently to our inner impulses, to the messages of the body, heart, mind and spirit.

WHY THIS BOOK?

Create your own method. Don't depend slavishly on mine.
Make up something that will work for you!
But keep breaking traditions, I beg you.
—*Constantin Stanislavski*

There are dozens of books on comedy improv available and some on physical theatre improvisation but very few focusing on dramatic, narrative improvisation. Several books I've found to be very valuable employ improvisation as acting training but offer no guidance concerning improvisation as performance. These two, by Steven Wangh and David Zinder, contain lots of improvisation exercises used in their acting classes.

I'm grateful for this wonderful book, *An Acrobat of the Heart* by Steven Wangh, of NYU (who I jammed with exactly once), which contains exercises similar to ones I've used for years (we both studied with Jerzy Grotowski's Polish Laboratory Theatre) and others I'd never heard of and have since adopted. I also love David Zinder's *Body, Voice, Imagination: A Training for the Actor*, which I've used to great benefit. Then there's the improv bible: Viola Spolin's *Improvisation for the Theater*, whose highly structured exercises work very well for children but which I use sparingly for adults. However, the Spolin book is so extensive that you can choose exercises from it and adapt them to use in nearly any style of improvisation. I've done that. And, of course, Keith Johnstone's much esteemed and very readable *Impro*, a font of fruitful exercises and philosophy.

I use some voice exercises I learned while studying Kristin Linklater's technique. Her book, *Freeing the Natural Voice*, describes this technique in depth. And I've been inspired by *Free Play: Improvisation in Life and Art* by musician, Stephen Nachmanovitch, a deeply thoughtful and poetic book of philosophy and narrative. In the 1970s Stephen would sometimes play his glorious violin music for improvised dance jams that I was in with Jani Novak, John Graham and others. I see my book as a complement to other books in the improvisation canon.

While it's impossible to learn any form of theatre exclusively from a book—theatre is a physical, collaborative form—I hope that the philosophy, principles and exercises offered here may be a support to students and teachers of improvisational theatre, as well as to all who long to expand their range of creative self-expression. The chapters may be read in any order, but the exercises are arranged fundamentals first, and may be used for all skill levels unless otherwise noted.

PLAY

Spontaneity and discipline, far from weakening each other, mutually reinforce themselves.

—*Jerzy Grotowski*

Like every grandma, I am blessed with the most delightful, brilliant, imaginative grandchildren in the world. I'm grateful to them for the joy they bring to my life and for demonstrating to me the naturalness of dramatic play. No one has to teach Maceo, or any four-year-old, how to pretend: how to growl, sing, dance, make sounds of a siren, plane, dog or jackhammer. Adults do not tell him how to transform a stick into a weed whacker, magic wand, or baseball bat or how to tell the story of his rescue, as a fireman, of children in danger, or the special place his imaginary train will take us.

To be artists, we need to cultivate the endless curiosity of children. Play is essential to human development, and not only humans: all mammals partake in play. Dramatic play is a natural activity that serves to help us understand and engage with the world. So, when a beginning student tells me, "I don't have any imagination," I say, "Well, you had one when you were four and, believe me, you have one now."

It's understandable that adults feel this way, given the less than welcoming attitude towards creativity that many of us have experienced in school. I, for one, mostly hated school (until I got to college) feeling that I was usually "wrong." Children, during the necessary process of being socialized, are told that certain behaviors are "inappropriate" (a euphemism for bad), that is: improper behavior for a particular situation. This may be a constructive strategy in social life, but in the arts, striving to be appropriate or polite is the kiss of death for the creative impulse. People often confuse being sensitive or caring with being polite.

I've taught children, teens and adults, but most often people between the ages of 20 and 80. When I teach children I don't use a lot of technique drawn from FSI. FSI, with its focus on release and opening, was developed for adults. Children, with their natural expressiveness, usually don't need release as much as structure, support and clarity, a container for their creative play,

According to Barry Shaw, a researcher at the University of California–Berkeley:

> In early childhood, distinct types of free play are associated with high creativity. Preschoolers who spend more time in role-play (acting out characters) have higher measures of creativity: voicing someone else's point of view helps develop their ability to analyze situations from different perspectives. When playing alone, highly creative first graders may act out strong negative emotions: they'll be angry, hostile, anguished. The hypothesis is that play is a safe harbor to work through forbidden thoughts and emotions. Unfortunately, the place where our first creative ideas go to die is the place that should be most open to them— school. Studies show that teachers overwhelmingly discriminate against creative students, favoring their classmates who more readily follow directions and do what they're told. Even if children are lucky enough to have a teacher receptive to their ideas, standardized testing and other programs like No Child Left Behind and Race to the Top (a program whose very designation is opposed to nonlinear creative thinking) make sure children's minds are not on the "wrong" path, even though adults' accomplishments are linked far more strongly to their creativity than their IQ. All of this negativity isn't easy to digest, and social rejection can be painful. But there is a glimmer of hope in all of this. A Cornell study makes the case that social rejection is not actually bad for the creative process—and

can even facilitate it. The study shows that if you have the sneaking suspicion you might not belong, the act of being rejected confirms your interpretation. The effect can liberate creative people from the need to fit in and allow them to pursue their interests.

Yay for the outsider! Yay for the creative impulse. Into adulthood, into old age, let's keep searching for our own path.

Will FSI make us children again? I don't think so. I hope not. Our play will be rich with the years of accumulated experience of adults: of observation, thought, learning, forgetting. We have knowledge of the shadow side of humanity, as well as the light. This art form strives to help us find the treasure in it all.

PATTI MEYER

AUTHENTICITY AND COLLABORATION

DEFINITION OF TERMS

For those new to the genre, here are some expressions you'll find throughout the book.

Physical life: Expression through the body

Verbal life: Expression through the use of a known language

Vocal life: Expression through the use of the voice, without words (sound)

Emotional life: Radiating feeling. Always present whether or not we're aware of it

Fourth wall: The imaginary wall that separates the performers from the audience. In stage directions, we have the upstage wall at the back of the stage, stage right wall (actors' right,) stage left (actors' left), and the downstage, invisible fourth wall, which in experimental improvisational theatre, is either very porous or, in solo performance, may not exist at all.

Beats: in acting, beats are defined as a unit of meaning: when emotional life changes, that's a beat change. For our purposes, when a new plot element is introduced we can also call that a new beat.

OFFERING AND ACCEPTING: THE HEART OF THE MATTER

In improvisational theatre, everything an actor does or says is considered an "offer." It is the responsibility—and pleasure—of the other actors to accept the offers that their fellow performers make; to not do so is known as blocking, or denial, which can prevent the piece from moving forward and can impede the connection between the actors. Accepting an offer is accompanied by adding a new offer, building on the earlier ones. The idea is to meet and respond to your partners where they are. Every new image, action, gesture, feeling or piece of information added, helps the players to progress the action of the piece.

In creating Full Spectrum Improvisational Theatre, one of the ongoing questions we embrace is, "How do I express myself authentically while connecting and co-operating with my partners?" This, of course, is a question that is alive in every relationship, on stage or off. Developing enough self-trust to be transparent is the path to emotional safety. We need to accept that all our emotions are equally valuable in theatre. If we can embrace our feelings, we can play them, we can use them as fodder for the piece we're building. An authentic offer is one that feels real and that involves some degree of self-revelation. Many exercises I use in training are designed to practice this: Self Intro-Three Ways, Three Claps, Connections, Singing to Invisible Other, Auto Bio Solo stories, Character from Worst/ Best Trait, I Feel, Let Your Partner Change You...

In improvisational jazz, the rules of conventional musical structure are often put aside in favor of creative instinct and intuition. When "mistakes" are seen as offers, rather than problems, we're in the improv groove, a magical place. In improvisational jazz there's a maxim: if you play the "wrong" note, play it again. It then becomes a choice to explore. Players are able to return to the home base of known structure whenever that is needed to uphold the artistic integrity of the music. FSI is like that.

We can think of ourselves as mediums for the stories and creative images coming through us, just welcoming them. We don't have to figure them out. We just do our best to get out of the way and let each piece show us what to do.

Everything is seen and heard by the audience and by your performance partners. If you meant to say one thing but said something different (as frequently happens on and off stage), what you actually said is what has been heard. If you meant to sound angry, but

PATTI MEYER

you realize it came out more as confused, then your character is confused, maybe confused and angry. Play that.

LET THE OFFER LAND

What does it mean to accept an offer? It means to hear it, to feel it, to be affected by it. And most important, to respond to it.

Example: At the top of a scene, after 20 seconds of wordless movement, A approaches B timidly from across the space, while fidgeting and nervously adjusting his clothing, and says, in a soft, quivering voice:

"I think we know each other from Cedar High."

That's a rich offer because A (Apple), with clear emotional and physical life, has let his partner and the audience know something about his character and he's implied a history between the characters. B (Banana) has a lot to work with and many choices as to how to respond.

Banana could look at Apple, livid with anger, and say:

"Oh my god, It's YOU!"

She could say nothing, look at him lovingly, grab him and kiss him passionately. She could take one look and run across the space, away from him, cowering, terrified. All strong responses. No one choice is better than the others. So, how does she know what to do? She responds from her impulse, driven by real feeling. Every gesture, movement, bit of text, vocal quality, or emotion triggers associations from real life in us. This is our material.

BLOCKING, CONSTRUCTIVELY AND NOT

If, in the above scenario, Banana semi-blocked the offer, it might look something like this:

A: I think we know each other from Cedar High.

B: (sharply) I never went to Cedar High.

Or

B: What are you talking about?

These responses from B could be used as stimulating offers, if we keep our imaginations open. If B's statement "I never went to Cedar High" was acted with the clear sub-text (unspoken feelings) that she's lying, it would be a juicy response. It's all in the delivery. Or B's "What are you talking about?" could show how she treated A (badly) when they did both go to Cedar High, justifying A's fear of her.

So, most responses can be seen as workable offers, though some are easier to work with than others. But here's a response that feels like a real block to me.

A: I think we know each other from Cedar High.

B: No, I don't think so. (delivered in a neutral tone)

This gives Apple very little. It's a stingy or "wimpy" response. Once we've learned how to accept and develop offers, we can choose to block or redirect some when necessary for authenticity or safety or for dramatic or comedic effect.

Sometimes we don't want to accept a particular offer because it feels phony or forced. I find that self-blocking is a more problematic habit among improvisers than blocking one's partner. I see players going politely along with an endowment or a scenario that they clearly don't believe in, to the great detriment of the work. The actors feel it. The audience feels it. It's very uncomfortable for all concerned.

The audience comes to a show to see actors reveal themselves, to be fearless and vulnerable. Of course, this takes courage. We need to develop our courage to live a full life as well as to create art.

When I studied with Keith Johnstone in the 1980s, he had us do a "Creative Blocking" exercise, in which we purposefully blocked every third or fourth offer. I really enjoyed the exercise and found that it kept the players very alert and the scenes quite lively. It also helped to avoid overly logical and predictable scenes, a particular peeve of mine. We can say "No, and..." refusing the offer but immediately making a counter-offer.

Example:

Apple says, "Go and stand on the chair." Banana, who doesn't feel safe standing on the chair may say, "You know I'm afraid of heights. You just wanna see me scared." Thus offering a little back-story and a possible conflict. Yes, the old saw that there is no drama without conflict does seem to hold true. We need obstacles in the way of characters getting what they want or we have no story. The exception would be theatre as ritual. More about that later in this book.

The blocking examples I've given are all verbal offers because we don't see as much inorganic physical behavior. It's much easier to be revealing and uniquely yourself when making physical offers. Improvisers have the option to respond to any offer, physical or verbal, with movement, gesture and/or sound. In fact, my first recommendation when an improviser is in trouble is to take a break from talking and express himself physically. We never want to use our energy to hide what we're feeling or to block material that's coming up for us. We want to commit ourselves to the process of revealing.

GENDER AND ISSUES OF MEANING AND POWER IN THEATRE

The issue of gender equality in improv ensembles comes up a lot in the world of comedy improv. Over time, my Full Spectrum Improvisation classes tend to have a pretty equal gender distribution. There are clearly more men doing comedy. Talking about sexism can arouse strong feelings. So, let's start with the observation that this is not, alas, a "post-sexist" society any more than it's a "post-racial" society.

KOSHO

I'll weigh in from the perspective of an actor who has spent much of a 45-year performing, teaching, directing career performing improvisation with women. I've also been in and directed many ensembles that included men. Safety on stage is always an issue. I often read online complaints by women improvisers about sexism in the world of improv, ranging from being groped or sexually assaulted by men improvisers to sexist scenarios. Here's an observation by Emily Schorr Lesnick, posted on Splitsider, an improv site:

> The dynamics of male improvisers bulldozing their female scene partners can limit their agency. A friend of mine, the only woman in a ten-person improv team that touted their cutting-age improv, entered an ongoing scene between two men. Her "walk-on" initiation was a clear assistant dropping off important papers to a supervisor, entering to say, "Here are your papers, boss," and then leaving. However, when she entered the scene, her male scene partner labeled her a prostitute, exclaiming "You must leave, sir, my prostitute is here!" Bad improv, yes. But let's dissect further:

> This line of dialogue made this improviser into the object of laughter (and, as a prostitute, an object of sexual desire) and destroyed her initiation into the scene as another character from the business setting. This improviser's adherence to rules of agreement in improv scenes effectively silenced her, as she negotiated her visible hurt and frustration with her desire to support her teammates. Male improvisers create and adhere to these rules of agreement while women sometimes have no choice but to go along with it. Moments like these present women with a choice to accept their status in an offensive joke and collude with oppression for the sake of teamwork, or risk disapproval from scene partners should they object.

This idea that you "have no choice but to go along with it" makes me want to tear my hair out. Of course you have a choice! Please, do not go along with trashy or humiliating offers for the sake of co-operation. Knuckling under does not create art. There are other options in performance and in life. You've got to take the YES, AND principle with a grain of salt. We should not slavishly obey "improv rules" that were not devised by us. We can speak up for our dignity and artistry when we find ourselves in the midst of a bigoted scenario.

In this instance, the female improviser in the above scene could choose the interpretation that, rather than endowing her character as a prostitute, her partner has endowed his character as a pig. She could oink at him. Or, she could say, in response to the prostitute endowment, "In your dreams, buddy." Or, with great dignity and high status: "Mr. Taylor, I must have misheard you. You didn't call me a prostitute, did you?" Or, she can react without words by simply turning and leaving the scene, (which is likely want she wanted to do, anyway.) She might accompany this action with a scream or a look of disdain thrown at the actor who spoke the offensive words. Or any number of other actions. If the male actor is the least bit resourceful, he will find a creative way to respond to her strong offers.

BREAKING THE FRAME

In FSI, the need for choice and individuality is highly honored. Responding to an offer that feels inorganic or offensive, we can also "Break the Frame," a technique in which the actor peels away the fictional reality of the scene to reveal her own reality.

Example: Five seconds into a piece, Actor A endows his scene partner as his lover by saying, in a leering voice, "I'm really looking forward to some alone time with you." Actor B is startled by this offer, as she doesn't see herself as actor A's girlfriend at all. It's so early into the scene that she hasn't yet discovered the nature of her relationship to A, and is just beginning to feel their emotional connection. She wants to avoid clichés of the "Honey, I'm home" variety, so responds honestly by saying "Oh, I'm your girlfriend?"

Actor A then has many options. He can use the offer as part of the fictional story: "Oh, come on, play house with me," or "Well,

you look just like her." Actor A can break the frame himself: "Hey, you're supposed to accept my offers," which opens up a discussion. B: "Yeah, but I don't feel like being your girlfriend or wife...unless we're about to split up." Or "I'm tired of that role. How about if I be the man this time?"

Lots of provocative possibilities and choices open up. The audience may be momentarily surprised, even apprehensive, witnessing the actors disagreeing, which will likely increase their engagement. Surprise is an essential aspect of the pleasure of improvisation for both audience and players.

The example above is drawn from a piece with one of my scene partners, Dan, who at one time, tended to see most female players in a romantic or sexual light. At our next rehearsal I asked him to try to see women on stage with him as anything but sex objects. (A sister, friend, ghost, boss, mother, part of himself, colleague…) He did that in subsequent shows with great success. But in this piece we actually jumped into a full-fledged, brief, but very dramatic argument about what we were doing, then, having decided to switch roles, we jumped back into the fictional scene with me as a macho man, wearing a man's jacket, and Dan as the girlfriend with a flowered scarf over his shoulders. It was risky but it worked beautifully. (Role reversal is also a well-known tool used in Psychodrama.) I enjoyed it immensely and so did Dan. And the audience applauded and laughed. They were thrilled to discover that Dan and I had the whole transaction under control. Of course, Dan and I knew each other well and understood the technique we were using. We felt confident that we could steer the piece in and out of the fictional world. This can produce a kind of meta-scene: that is, theatre about theatre, as well as referring to a larger reality.

In the above scenario, the initial problem may have been avoided if both players had postponed speech until an emotional connection was established. But once the problem emerges, Breaking the Frame can help. In this advanced technique, the actor is stepping out of the fictional role she is playing and telling the audience, or her partners, what's in her mind and heart. Breaking the frame is used as a tool in the quest for authenticity and as a way to "save" a failing piece. The actor may make a request of his partner, i.e.: "Let's start this piece over" or "Let's switch roles" (as above with Dan and Joya). Breaking the frame can also be used in the form of direct address to the audience: "Here I am playing the mother again, when I'd rather be the femme fatale," or a confession to the audience, "I have no idea what's going on. It's like they (the partners) are in one world and I'm in another." Good information for all scene partners to have. She may then return to the fictional character and setting of the piece or change it entirely. The idea is to name the actual inner life and relational dynamics of the players, to be totally self-revealing (a commonality with psychodrama). This easy moving in and out of fiction is a core stylistic marking of FSI. The need to break the frame doesn't come up often if improvisers are working organically, though it can be used for fun and to create surprise and complexity.

Also, in an ensemble performance, players may merge their actual reality with the fictional reality, as in this exchange: Screaming like a petulant child at her partners: "You're not looking at me." an actor is daring to tell the truth by identifying the reality between the players. Her partners get this and respond honestly, turning to look at her.

FULL SPECTRUM IMPROVISATION | 2:29

TEACHING PHILOSOPHY AND APPROACH
PLUS FEEDBACK, COACHING, & CRITIQUE
SKILL

> *An understanding heart is everything in a teacher,*
> *and cannot be esteemed highly enough.*
> *One looks back with appreciation to the brilliant teachers,*
> *but with gratitude to those who touched our human feeling.*
> *The curriculum is necessary raw material,*
> *but warmth is the vital element.*
>
> —*Carl Jung*

've spoken with improvisation teachers who say proudly that improv has a "low threshold," that anyone can do it, since we improvise every day in ordinary life, and that, for an audience, the pleasure in watching improvisation is in seeing the players confront the unknown, witnessing the spontaneous moment of creation. I get that perspective. I see the truth in it.

But it's also true that most "normal" individuals' range of behavior in everyday life can be quite limited. It's usually much narrower than the behaviors accepted in the socially sanctioned schizophrenia that is theatre. There may be very little spontaneity or originality. Theatre training should expand our range of behaviors and actions way beyond the everyday.

Some kinds of short-form comedy improv, based on simple games and gimmicks, are easy to do (if you have the temperament for it) and can be learned in a few lessons. But as an audience member, I don't enjoy seeing just "anyone" perform. When I go to the theatre and pay for my ticket I want to see skilled players creating artful performances, improvised or not.

That said, the reality is that in most improvisation classes outside of universities and professional acting schools, many students don't intend to become professional performers. I've asked a half-dozen improv teachers; they agree. It's a hard life, trying to support oneself through theater work and nearly impossible to earn sufficient income from improvised shows, no matter how often you perform. Students may be in class for other reasons: recreation, personal creative growth, fun, social connections. All great reasons to study improvisation.

Still, the "low threshold" concept can easily lead to low expectations of students and training that is not as artful or rich or therapeutic as it can be. Which brings us to the difference between improvisational theatre as art and improvisation as therapy.

Renee Emunah, in her big book about drama therapy, *Acting for Real*, remarks that the most authentically felt and self-revealing acting also makes for the most artistically satisfying theatre. I agree with that, but only to a point. When we bring our performance to a paying audience, the goal of the work takes a turn away from being an activity primarily (or entirely) for the benefit of the participants. As performers, our job is to inspire, entertain, and/or educate, even to disturb, our audience. We actors often gratefully experience catharsis or healing as a by-product of the performance, but that's not our primary goal. We want the audience to feel that they are in good hands, that they can trust the performer to be in control of what happens, so that they, the audience, can relax and experience some kind of transformation. This requires skill. Improvising actors need a "bag of tricks" to elevate the artfulness of any piece and to make something of substance.

In class, I encourage students to use personal history as theatre material if the experience has been psychologically resolved. You need a certain distance from material that is emotionally painful. The experience has to be digested. Constantin Stanislavski (1863-1938), the director of Russia's Moscow Art Theatre and creator of the Stanislavski Method (Method Acting, as it's called, is mostly what's taught in American acting schools), said the event you're remembering, to trigger emotion, needs to have happened at least seven years ago. That's an arbitrary number, but you get the idea. It has to be something that you have some control over, but that still

arouses feeling. This is markedly different than the way life issues are approached in drama therapy, where the "acting out" of life dilemmas is done for the purpose of encountering and possibly resolving those issues.

In performance training I often use phrases of Sanford Meisner's (a famous American acting teacher): "Let your partner play you like an instrument." "Take everything your partner says personally." This is great advice for drama, while in stark contrast to what our couples' counselor told my husband and me: "Your partner's moods and actions are usually not about you. Don't always take them personally."

Many exercises used in drama therapy are drawn from improv theatre or acting technique. We use similar structures and tweak them for the purposes of facilitating psychological growth or to create performance art. The creative process itself and the expanding of self-expression are intrinsically therapeutic. It provides safe release for pent-up emotions, engages the whole psychophysical self, models many ways to connect with others, and expands participants' self-awareness and self-image. When creative movement is in the mix, there are clear changes in brain chemistry, such as the release of endorphins and dopamine, which are said to lift mood.

Acting training involves each person's ability to access and portray every conceivable emotion. If you don't cry, scream, show tenderness, and so on in real life, you can't do it convincingly on stage. In acting training you can learn to experience all emotions as aliveness, as vibrant energy, which can be guided and channeled by choice, accessing and expressing feelings in class that can then be accessed more easily in life. All our acting training is preparation so we can get to the point where we are living and responding in the moment.

I agree with the well-known axiom, originating with Meisner, "Acting is living truthfully under imaginary circumstances," and his view that acting should be "firmly rooted in the instinctive."

Therapists who study FSI training tell me that it's helpful in their clinical practice. The work may help to sharpen powers of observation and intuition, perhaps expanding awareness of nonverbal elements in their clients' behavior. The therapists themselves need an outlet for their own creative self-expression. They need to play, to laugh, to act wild and silly and angry and confused.

According to a 2015 Atlantic article, "So Funny It Doesn't Hurt," by Kathleen Toohill:

> For some, the benefits of improvisation can be significant: Researchers and clinical psychologists alike have begun to pay attention to improv, conducting studies or incorporate it into work with their patients. The improv stage, in theory, is a space free of judgment or fear of failure, making it an ideal environment for people who struggle with low self-esteem, social anxiety, or other types of anxiety disorders. "It will either turn out better than they thought, or if it doesn't go well, they will learn that they can cope. While not a substitute for therapy, some psychologists believe improv can be an effective complement, in part because of the way it mirrors the patient/therapist dynamic. In 2013, Gordon Bermant, a psychology professor at the University of Pennsylvania, published a paper in the journal *Frontiers in Psychology* that outlined the similarities between improv and applied psychology, or the use of psychological research to solve real-world problems. "Both improv and applied psychology practices aim to increase personal awareness, interpersonal attentiveness, and trust," he wrote. The lack of planning and structure in improv means that performers must function without a safety net, but, as Bermant noted in his paper, "If all play is relating authentically to each other, fear of failure loses its sting—a net of support is constructed from the openness, trust, and acceptance." The relationship among members of

an improv ensemble hinges on trust, as does the relationship between therapist and patient. "The idea of a therapist holding a client in 'unconditional positive regard' describes a way of relating to others which is close to the 'yes, and' affirmations of improv," Bermant says. A key tenet of therapy is the guarantee that the therapist will not judge the client for what he or she says.

Let's admit it, teaching is itself a performance. It should be an engaging and lively one. The teacher/director often demonstrates a skill (as in movement and vocal exercises) as well as modeling improvisational behavior by adapting the lesson to the group's needs moment by moment. I usually make a list of exercises before class but often diverge from that plan as the class progresses. And I let the students know that I am doing that. The list is comforting to have as a backup in case the muse is not with me. For new teachers, more preparation is a good idea.

RULES vs. PRINCIPLES

I love structure, technique and artistic principles. These are meant to enhance and guide the creative process, to give us a container in which to explore freely. I don't love rules. To me, the very word implies inflexibility and judgment. We need to avoid rules that tend to encourage conformity and compel players to be in the logical mind. Games have rules. Art doesn't. Games are helpful to create play, so there are games among the warm-ups and exercises in this book. Performances are not games.

I hear over and over again from my students, "Am I doing it right?" "Am I following the rules?" They report that these doubts, coming from rules they have been taught by previous teachers, haunt their minds and inhibit their impulses during performance.

Here's a sample of these "rules" encountered in comedy improv classes and books.

- **Don't ask questions.** (Well, that would forbid the first utterance in the scene I describe at the beginning of this book.

Can you imagine telling a playwright not to have questions in her script?)

- **Always say yes.** (This forbids creative blocking and can result in lots of inauthentic and shallow improvisation.)

- **Don't do teaching scenes.** (I get this one. Teaching scenes can be very predictable but they don't have to be, as long as the activity of teaching something morphs into a more complex relationship between student and teacher. I remember a very entertaining scene in my advanced group in which the teenage student became the dominant character and got the teacher to gleefully help him burn down the school.)

- **Don't play "drunk" or "stoned."** (Though we use it sparingly, the technique of playing drunk or stoned has proven useful when there is a need for a drastic character change. As a matter of fact, I keep a dull plastic syringe in my prop basket. We've had some gripping pieces that included shooting up. Also, the use of imaginary potions can create myriad possibilities. See section on playing drunk, cross gender and various ages in Chapter Five.)

- **Don't play a small child.** (Jim and Jacqueline, students in an advanced workshop, did a darkly comic scene in which 50-year-old Jim played a child of about four to Jacqueline's oppressive mother. The image of this strong, muscular man being dominated by a smaller woman was very powerful.)

Students should not be made to feel wrong, even when they're unclear on the instruction. I had a wonderful movement teacher, John Graham, who, when asked to repeat his instruction, would often say, "Do what you think you heard." This attitude addressed the anxiety to do it "right," the need to please the teacher that most students bring with them from a lifetime of other-directed behavior. Graham's attitude of permissiveness supported an atmosphere of free experimentation. That said, confusion about the structure (What is this exercise?) could be an impediment to concentration and engagement. It's often best just to repeat the instruction.

When I studied Creative Body Alignment, the work of Mabel Elsworth Todd of THE THINKING BODY and Kristin Linklater's voice work, I learned that the language that we use has a profound effect on our psycho-physical responses. For example: if you tell a person to straighten her back, you'll likely trigger a contraction in the back muscles. That's not what you want, so you say: "Let the back lengthen and widen," which is what you actually want. I think the word "rules" can cause a contraction in the imagination.

Another familiar rule of improv, "Make your partner look good," is not a phrase used in FSI, as I've found that suggesting that to students can encourage politeness. We try not to concern ourselves with the issue of anyone "looking good." When improv teachers say, "Make your partner look good," or "Think of your partner as a genius," they mean "Support and respect your partners and help them out if they're stuck." Why not say that?

NONIE KIMPITAK

I pass this list out to all new students (slightly amended for team-building or public-speaking classes).

Some attitudes and principles helpful for creating Improvisational Theatre and other art / life activities

- Take time every day to move, to daydream, to let your imagination roam freely.
- Get out in nature whenever possible.
- Stay present in your body, letting your sensory awareness inform you.
- Relax and allow the joy of play.
- Trust your intuition and don't worry about what you think the world (or the class or the teacher) expects of you.
- Cultivate your curiosity, your fearlessness and your fierceness.
- Get to know your "inner critic" and learn to identify his/her voice. Practice co-existing with the critic without being dominated by him/her/them.
- Think of your creative work as an experiment and be good-natured about the process.
- Commit yourself fully to whatever you are doing. Give yourself over to what the work needs.
- Connect and co-operate with your partners. Be willing to lead or follow.
- Listen with your ears, body, eyes, soul.
- Take risks and be willing to make "mistakes." There are no "right" or "wrong" choices, just skillful and less skillful.
- Tell the truth, emotionally, verbally and physically.
- It won't help to try to be "original" or "funny." That tends to trigger the inner critic. Who knows what "original" is, anyway?
- Stay in the moment and trust the moment, as much as possible.
- Let the physical & emotional life lead you to the verbal life of any piece/story.
- Keep a journal about your creative work.

COMMITMENT

While beginning students may not be giving much thought to long-term goals in theatre, most advanced students are honing their skills with an aim to performance. When I hear from advanced students that they can't come to class because they have a sore neck or haven't been getting enough sleep or have to pack for vacation, I'd like them to remember commitment to the creative life. It isn't easy, but to live a creative life we must nurture our passion, regardless of the circumstances. We can't wait to create art until we're in our best form, until we feel rested and secure, because those moments are few and far between. Sometimes we just have to muscle through. Good work often comes out of sessions when we were least expecting it. I don't give this advice to students at the moment they cancel, because guilt-tripping is worse than useless. But I look for moments in class when I can mention it.

FLOW

The duration of exercises can be decided on the spot, and intuitively, by the leader, who will sense when the purpose of any given exercise has been satisfied. Try to end the exercise when you feel all (or almost all) have gotten it, before participants' focus begin to wander, and definitely before boredom or restlessness develops. When you have a rich knowledge of many exercises, you can draw on them in the moment to address learning needs that arise spontaneously.

The way one exercise flows into the next is important in training. We want to maintain concentration and immersion in the work. We want a sense of one activity triggering another, as when in performance we want a sense of the relationship of each scene or solo to the other pieces, a sense of the whole.

As teachers and directors gain experience, we begin to understand how and when to give feedback or critique to students with differing levels of skill and in differing emotional conditions. When working with students with physical limitations, help them to feel comfortable doing what they can. This is not ballet. It's not necessary to be athletic or young to do FSI. There are many ways to fulfill an exercise or structure.

STUCK?

Here's a list I hand out to Intermediate/Advanced students.

WHAT TO DO WHEN STUCK (IN PERFORMANCE)

- Let it be all right. Enjoy being in your senses and your body.
- Let your heart and mind stay open while waiting attentively for the next impulse.
- Focus on your connection with your partner(s).
- Feel the audience's support; know they are with you.
- Do what your partner is doing.
- Use rhythm and repetition. Repeat (re-wind) what you, or your partner, just did.
- Reveal. Tell the truth – physically, emotionally, verbally, to your partner(s) and/or
- "Break the Frame" and confess to the audience.
- Intensify your feeling and physicalize it—great confusion, go mute, stutter-stammer, speak gibberish, sing, etc. Play the character you are at this moment (very shy, vulnerable, scared, giddy, blustery, excited, paranoid?)
- WHAT IF YOU FEEL YOUR PARTNER HAS BLOCKED YOU?
- Repeat your offer; make sure she's heard and/or seen you.
- The "block" is an offer. Respond to it.
- Make a new offer that's physical (non-verbal).
- "Break the Frame"; talk to your partner as your fellow actor or address the audience.
- Live fully in your own reality and follow your path/through line. Find a task to do.
- Live parallel to your partner, without inter-acting.

COACHING A STUCK PLAYER

Notes from class:

Jeff is in the middle of an improvised piece. He stops:

Jeff: I don't know what to do right now. I'm blank. There's nothing going on.

Joya: There's always something going on. Usually when improvisers say their mind is blank, what's really happening is that they're judging and blocking the impulse that's there, obstructing the path of action. What did you want to do at that moment?

Jeff: I dunno. Well, maybe I wanted to run away.

Joya: Ah. You can do that, within the scene.

Jeff: I can?

Joya: Yup. It's an offer. You can also tell your scene partner, "I feel like running away."

Jeff: OK.

Joya: What's happening in your body right now?

Jeff: Uh…I feel kind of tense.

Joya: (smiling) Yes. Your hands are clenched.

Jeff: Oh, yeah. (laughs)

Joya: That's fine—you can use it. Let it play through your whole body, exaggerate it, intensify it. Let the sensations move you.

Jeff closes his eyes and allows the feeling in his hands to begin to play through his whole body. It is fascinating to watch. With coaching, gradually he begins to transform. His chest caves in, and his spine is curved. His fingers become gnarled. His face, normally boyish, crumples, and a curious being begins to appear. His breathing becomes loud and raspy. His scene partner, who has been watching carefully, moves slowly into his space. He looks at her. She snarls at him. Together they develop characters and a relationship within a poetic story. Jeff found his way forward by going back to the body.

DE-BRIEFING

After each performance in class and after some exercises, we applaud, a supportive and celebratory act. And we de-brief. I ask the improvisers, "What was that like for you?" I want to know the players' experience of their work before I comment because I want to respect their reality. The teacher or director may also ask some (not all) of these questions:

- What did you notice?
- Did any questions arise?
- How was your connection with your partners?
- When did you feel the most at ease?
- When did you feel tension or struggle?
- Why do you think that happened?
- Is there something you wanted to do or say that you held back?
- What happened there...? (If you pause the scene and want them to reflect on a specific moment)

FOR WITNESSES (FELLOW STUDENTS) IN CLASS:

- What did you enjoy about that piece?
- Were you engaged most of the time? If not, when was that?
- Is there something you wanted more or less of?

FEEDBACK FOR BEGINNERS

In Beginner classes I give little corrective feedback, except for students who've been studying for a while and for who I've gotten to know how they handle critique. Mostly, I look for what worked and talk about why it worked. Unless beginners ask for critique, I mainly offer lots of encouragement. I trust that over time they will develop skill and, with skill, more confidence and ease. It can be useful, however, if students feel they have failed, to investigate their thinking about that. What went wrong? Did they express truthfully what was in their minds and bodies? Much of the time, if concentration is off, it's because of the distraction of the inner critic's voice. Often students do not give themselves credit for what

did work in the improvisation, focusing on deficit instead of abundance.

Having the players speak the critic's words out loud can be very informative for all. Actors can open a conversation between the inner critic and their artist selves, playing both roles.

You can check books about Psychodrama and Voice Dialogue (a mode of growth psychology related to Jungian theory) such as *Embracing Your Inner Critic* by Drs. Hal and Sidra Stone, for specific exercises on addressing self-doubt.

FEEDBACK FOR INTERMEDIATE / ADVANCED PLAYERS

Leading these exercises requires tact, sensitivity, patience and lots of compassion. Students may cry. We don't make a big deal of it. Students may cry while doing other exercises, as well. It should be made clear that tears are a natural and appropriate response to certain stimuli and each person will have their personal emotional triggers. We value tears as much as laughter. In fact there are exercises in this book that may invite crying. (Singing to Invisible Other, Solo Stories From Life, Solo from Best and Worst Character Traits…) Actors, of course, need to learn how to cry on stage and to be able to control their tears, so that they are not overwhelmed by emotion when performing.

Intermediate/Advanced students want and need critique of their technique and observations about their habits. Advanced students often benefit from being challenged by their teacher. Always start feedback with what's working well. It's well known that most people will be more open to constructive criticism if they first hear something positive about their work. If there's an area of challenge, you may want to offer an exercise that addresses that aspect of the work, i.e.: Physical and Emotional Life First for someone who spends a lot of time in scenes standing and talking, or an objective such as "searching for tenderness" for an actor who usually plays aggressive characters.

Kindness and compassion must be a part of all critiques. When I studied directing with Joseph Chaikin of The Open Theatre, I was struck by him saying, "You must never take away your actors' courage."

It's fruitful to have advanced students critique each other and to have them practice side coaching and directing. For those who want to learn to teach FSI themselves, this is essential. And for all improvisers, directing sharpens their observation skills and helps them understand the craft. Along with developing our artist's intuition, we want to develop our understanding of how technique works.

Occasionally, it's useful to both student and teacher for the teacher to play directly with advanced students in a scene. At times, though rarely, when it looks to me like the actors are not connecting and I'm not sure how to help them, I'll jump in and very briefly take a player's place onstage in order to feel what it's like to play with each actor. I've found this illuminating and clarifying.

THE CRITIC, SKILL AND INSPIRATION

I've also often noticed this phenomenon in class: After performing with partners or solo, when I ask the students how it was for them, some will tell me that their critic was up, big time, criticizing many of their choices. Often I'm able to see the students' discomfort. But sometimes their work looks competent to me and to the other students, even when the players are uncomfortable. Improvisers who carry on and keep re-focusing on the task at hand with skill will produce decent improvised pieces, even while suffering from negative self-judgment. They're working technically—and may not be having much fun (the work will be better when they are)—but we cannot always be inspired.

"THE REACTION"

Students have also reported a phenomenon that has come to be called "The Reaction." When they've done something particularly revealing in class or made what they considered a big mistake, they feel very embarrassed a day or so later. Sometimes this feeling makes them not want to return to class. Happily for me, Bob, the student who first told me about this painful regret, was a committed improviser who came back to class the next week and talked about it. As you might guess, he found others in class who'd had this experience. I bring it up in class now and then, asking, "Did anyone have The Reaction this week?"

HABITS AND INTERVENING

What aid can we find to combat habit? The opposed habit? If you like doing something, do it regularly; if you don't like doing something, make a habit of doing something different.

—Epictetus

Collaboration reveals habits of interpersonal behavior. Players are reminded to notice patterns that are repeated. For example: "Oh, I almost always (or never) lead the scene." "I find myself yelling and angry every time I'm in a scene with women." "I always play the caregiver in scenes." "I tend to go along with whatever is offered even when I really don't want to." It's great to have these observations so that limitations can be addressed.

When teaching or directing, try to notice blocking and to intuit "hurt feelings" and encourage players to reveal feelings in class so they may receive support and all may learn from these occasions.

For the sake of creative growth, it can be effective for the teacher/

director to interrupt acting that is clearly (in the teacher's judgment) not organic or aligned with the student's wellbeing, such as playing characters they feel under-skilled to play or with whom they feel no connection. An intervention would be useful in an exercise where a student is looking around to see if the teacher is watching. With the intention of putting the student at ease, the teacher may redirect students' focus to the experience, rather than the appearance of what she's doing. We don't want anyone to practice non-productive behaviors. We want the improviser to learn to recognize the feeling of "trying to please" so that she can choose to change her behavior. Awareness creates choice.

ART AND REALITY

> *The greatest wisdom is to realize one's lack of it.*
>
> —*Constantin Stanislavski*

I encourage students to make strong offers, to take risks, and to trust that their partners are able to take care of themselves creatively and emotionally. We spend time in class exploring how to do that with sensitivity and care by focusing on the connection between players. This relationship is where we'll find the "story" of the piece, in collaboration with our partners.

After performing, a new student says, "That felt real to me, so that's not acting, right?"

I have to smile, thinking of the many acting classes I've attended and taught where students were working to "feel real" or, actually, to be real. In improvisational theatre, as in all acting, when creating fictional realities and characters we are in the territory of me / not me, real /not real.

We often discover aspects of ourselves that we don't know well. The resemblance of improvisation to real life creates a unique situation when it comes to distinguishing one's acting emotions from real feelings. They are all real feelings. But we work to develop an enhanced ability to control and direct them. To make art out of them.

Sometimes we must remind ourselves (or be reminded) that we are playing. As actors, we need to have open access to our whole emotional palette and to accept that all our feelings are valuable as dramatic material. We need willingness to be transparent, to drop our pretenses, within the bounds of safety, and to be agenda free. We need to be able to laugh at ourselves. And we need to commit to the process. Thoughts, feelings, and impulses occur when improvising that we may judge as "not appropriate" in the piece. If the improviser accepts these thoughts as offers instead of judging them, they can provide material for the piece. The "not appropriate" judgment often turns out to be applied to content that is not logical or that we are afraid to reveal—often the most surprising and interesting material.

In FSI we're not trying to create a "well-made play." Our style is less linear and can be more abstract than naturalistic drama, though the reality of our emotional expression was brought home to me in an incident during a summer intensive in Marin County.

It was July and very hot, so we had all windows and doors open. The classes went on all day, from 10 to 5, and afternoons we practiced scenes and solos.

Three actors were in the middle of an intense dramatic scene when a uniformed policeman appeared in our doorway, hand on his holster. I immediately stopped the scene and asked the cop, "May I help you, officer?"

He looked around a moment and said with real curiosity, "What are you doing?"

Me: This is an acting workshop, improvisational theatre, actually. These actors are in the middle of a scene.

Cop: Oh. Your neighbors complained that there was yelling and swearing going on and it sounded violent.

Me: (Feeling nervous) I'm sorry, we can close the doors to dampen the sound. Please reassure the neighbors that all is well here. It's just play, really.

Cop: Yeah, sure. Do you have a brochure or something? (I hand him a flyer, which he reads, then looks up). Ya know, I've always been interested in acting. Maybe I'll take a class sometime.

Me: Love to have you.

Cop: You go ahead with your work. No problem. I'll handle the neighbors.

Me: Thank you.

After he left, the group burst into applause.

HANDLING "DIFFICULT" STUDENTS

Every now and then, teachers will need to deal with a student who is hostile and disruptive or one who just seems dissatisfied with most class activities. In these upsetting situations our first reaction as teachers may be to feel hurt and defensive. When I'd been teaching only a few years, my first response was often anger. (How dare this person disrupt my class!?) Over time and after studying Nonviolent Communication, I realized that I'd have to work on my reaction so that I could protect the class from toxic energy coming from both the miserable student and myself. I also needed to model creative ways to handle conflict, as this is an important skill—in class, in ensemble and in life. Here are my suggestions:

As soon as you can, take the person aside (usually you can do that at a break) and tell her that you'd like to meet one on one after class, or as soon as a meeting can be arranged. When you meet, see if you, the teacher, can listen with genuine curiosity. Ask what needs are not being met in class for her. And what needs are being met. At check-in time, you heard a bit about what the student wants to get out of class but you need to go deeper because sometimes a student expects your class to "change his life" or he expects more personal attention than you are willing or able to give.

The person will need empathy (we all do), which is hard to give when you feel threatened. The teacher needs to understand the reason for the rebellious behavior. It may have little to do with you. In most situations of this kind that I've encountered, the student brought with them disappointment, confusion, anger or pain with which they were living. I found that, though I often wanted to address their suffering, my class was set up to do that only in a very limited way.

If you are a new teacher who feels insecure about your skills, you may be tempted to "pull rank," that is, to take an authoritarian stance. Do your best to resist this impulse. It's not constructive and will cause more rebellion in the student. The class may simply not be a good fit. If this is the case, suggest either a different class or suggest the person drop out and offer to refund tuition for the remaining classes.

A few times over the years, I've had to ask students to leave class when I was unable to come to an understanding with them and felt their presence was destructive to the mission of the work or to the emotional or physical safety of the other students. If you do have to ask someone to leave, say it as clearly and calmly as you can, explaining that as he seems unhappy with the class it makes sense for him to drop out. One student argued angrily with me and I had to tell him that I was uncomfortable having him in class. That was certainly the truth.

You may also use this encounter as an opportunity to improve your teaching. The student may have something useful to say about your class. In this case, you may want to apologize and promise to make a change in your approach. I've learned a great deal from students who are willing to talk openly with me about their experience in my classes.

I've enjoyed the work of many skillful performers in my advanced classes. Usually they are generous with other students but occasionally I'll have a talented actor (I'm using the word "talented" here but I avoid using it in class) who feels frustrated that many of the other improvisers in class don't have his level of experience. I tell him that I'll make a point of coaching him more rigorously. And I acknowledge him for the professional performer he is by asking if he would enjoy leading some of the warm-ups or possibly offering the group a challenging exercise or two. In most cases the answer was yes. All were happy to learn something new, and the actor's frustration dropped away.

Here's another little story that exemplifies a great way to solve a "discipline problem" with a student. Yes, it's about preschoolers (my grandson, forgive me), not adults, but the commitment to finding a creative solution applies. Maceo, at four and a half years old, was in his last year of preschool. His school had a rule about naptime. All the children, even the older ones like Maceo who no longer took naps, had to lie down on their mats in the darkened nap room for twenty minutes before they were allowed to get up and go play quietly in the other rooms. The teachers hoped some of the older children would fall asleep. And some did. Not Maceo. He lay awake, trying to be patient, waiting for the moment when he would be free to go out into the light. This particular day his patience didn't hold for the full twenty minutes and he got up after ten minutes and headed for the door. The teacher in charge, vigilant, got up and blocked the door with her body. Actually a teacher's aide, she was the youngest and least experienced at the school. She felt she had to enforce the rule. This led to a heated argument, in whispers, which, because of her greater stature, the young woman won. Maceo sat, seething, for another five or six minutes, then got up and left quickly while the teacher's aide was tending to another child. He was discovered by Miss Sophie, the head teacher, in the "Property Room," where he was in the process of methodically moving down the line of neatly arranged children's shoes and spitting in each one. I know this story because Miss Sophie, after interrupting Maceo's rebellious act, later called my son and daughter-in-law to report the incident. She also reported how she resolved it. Miss Sophie and Maceo had a serious conversation in which he was chastised for spitting and in which he apologized. She listened attentively while Maceo made his case for future liberation from the twenty-minute nap room rule. Miss Sophie's solution, which I find brilliantly creative, was to give Maceo the task of helping the toddlers go to sleep by going from child to child and rubbing their little backs. Maceo welcomed this assignment as it empowered him and acknowledged his "big kid" status. It also kept him in the nap room, happily, for ten or twelve minutes. When my son told me about it, I was intrigued by the "performance art" aspect of my grandson's spitting activity. We got a laugh out of the story but did not laugh in front of Maceo.

STAGE FRIGHT / PERFORMANCE ANXIETY

We have met the enemy and he is us.

—Pogo

We need to be seen, to be heard, and to be recognized. One of the most obvious benefits of participating in carefully taught theatre training is the altering of the experience of being seen. When a person feels the attention of the audience as empathy, it is a transforming experience, a kind of victory over fear. It creates an amazing "high." I'm privileged to have seen, and felt, this transformation many times.

Still, we're all familiar with the pervasive, nerve-wracking fear of public speaking and performance that is suffered by many people. The fear of being witnessed is the fear of being judged and found inadequate. It's a fundamental human need to be accepted by our community. People talk about wanting to disappear, to become invisible, when in front of an audience. There is a profound and corrosive sense of shame that we have not lived up to our own or others' expectations of us. That we may "make a fool of our self."

Desperate to find some sense of safety, we may hold on to an agenda and become unavailable to our partners or the audience. We may be so afflicted that we must leave the stage. For students, I suggest that they may need to tolerate this discomfort for a while until they've acquired enough skill to feel that they have some control of the situation.

A PHOBIA

When we look closely at stage fright we see that it's a phobia: an "unreasonable fear." We think we'll be shunned by our community: by all in the room, the theatre world, the workplace, if our performance is not absolutely gripping, intelligent and entertaining. Is this shunning idea actually true or is it just a thought? As a performer who has received both positive and negative reviews and has messed up on stage, forgetting whole pages of text in well-rehearsed plays—or feeling creatively blocked in an improvised performance, I can tell you that, while being embarrassed, I have never been shunned.

If you have suffered embarrassment, you know that you won't really die from it. You'll recover. In fact, in most cases, an audience, whether made up of colleagues, friends, or strangers, is ready to give us support. They've come to the theatre/conference/gathering to have a good time. They're usually on your side.

Sometime during my twenties, I developed claustrophobia. Most of the time it was mild, but during pregnancy it became acute. I was terrified to take an elevator or spend time in any small windowless room. This was especially awkward as most public restrooms are small and windowless. After a few years of suffering the restrictions of this unreasonable fear, I enrolled in a 12-week phobia desensitization group with a psychotherapist and learned that phobias are a spillover of held anxiety and that avoiding the feared situation doesn't reduce the fear, it perpetuates it. With the therapist's support we talked about our phobias and we faced them by riding elevators and standing in dark closets holding the therapist's hand. We learned positive self-talk, re-assuring ourselves that we are safe. We monitored our breathing and the tension in our muscles. The treatment was quite effective. Though I still don't like four-foot-by-four-foot bathrooms or elevators, I use them frequently with no apparent damage. This phobia provided me with material: I wrote a short, solo theatre piece, Irma at the Movies, in which the protagonist is having a panic attack in a dark movie theatre.

PERFECTIONISM

Here's my response to a student who was bothered by a persistent voice telling him he had to be "The best."

Isn't that what most of us want? To be "The best?" Well, at least the competitive ones amongst us. The habit of comparing ourselves to others and constantly assessing who's "better" is deeply entrenched in our culture. The toxic idea that some of us are "winners" and others "losers" is very prevalent in our hyper-capitalist society. Oh,

the great relief when we allow ourselves to release from judgment and to ask ourselves what "best" is anyway. Doesn't that depend on who you're asking?

You have the need for approval, but you also have the need to be in touch with your creativity in your own inner life. It's a matter of balance. Of course you want to be a success, but the trick is to be so engaged with what you're doing that the external focus fades a little. Or a lot. The need for outside approval begins to recede because the need for your own self-expression is so strong. This needs to be the case with small theatre because we're not on Broadway, we're not in the movies, there's not likely going to be millions of people loving us. You just have to really, bottom line, do it because you need to do it and you love to do it. And if you bring that love with you to the theatre, (or to any work or relationship in your life) the audience is going to feel it.

A LOOP OF LIGHT

It's a matter of shifting the focus. Is it out there or is it in here? I think of it really physically. In the warm-ups we do, we have a central vertical axis. When I'm preparing to go on stage, I really am checking into my own center, my own core; that I'm connected to that, so my energy is not being dissipated. We have images we can use when performing, to stay connected to the present moment. One of them is feeling a loop of energy between yourself and the audience. I see it visually: a loop of light. We're connecting. I send energy to them and they send it to me. You can call it love, you can call it whatever you want, it's just energy. It's not that you're ever blocking them out. They're right there with you. That's part of your world in theatre. There's that connection. But you don't have to give the audience a lot of power.

The relationship between performer and audience, especially in comedy, can be fraught with adversarial and threatening language: "I died last night (on stage)." "I killed." "I bombed." "I knocked 'em dead." The loop of light image helps defeat these damaging metaphors.

You can never really know what an audience member is thinking. You can project your own thoughts on to them, but the truth is, you don't know. That man in the back who keeps staring at the floor, the woman in the corner with her eyes closed. You may think they are bored or disgusted, but in fact they could be in a state of deep listening. They could be worried about something that has nothing to do with you. I remind my students of the pleasure and excitement of being witnessed, of the possibility of feeling empowered by the audience. We can learn to make the stage our home, a place of strength for us.

COURAGE

Creating theatre from scratch, with no script, can be daunting, as well as being great fun. In addition to skill, it requires courage and an open heart, mind and body. In class we often talk about why the experience of being in front of an audience is so harrowing for so many people.

During my many years of teaching and performing improvisational theatre it's often struck me that while many people I've encountered are afraid of performing, along with the fear there is often a passion and need for self-expression. And these two forces release a creative intensity in those willing to follow their passion in spite of their fear.

If it's managed, performance anxiety can be an asset, a source of energy. Interestingly, the physical sensations of stage fright are similar to those felt in a state of great excitement. Although it's the thoughts and images we hold that create anxiety, the symptoms are felt in the body: altered breathing, accelerated heart rate, dry mouth, sweating, maybe even shaking. I like to think of stage fright and excitement as being on the same emotional spectrum, just at opposite ends. In fact, it is useful to be in a heightened emotional state on stage, where a little extra adrenaline can provide energy and alertness. It's a matter of degree. I also think of each show as part of an ongoing learning process. There will be another day, another show. My life will not be destroyed by a less than stellar show. Nor will it be transformed by one terrific performance.

Although competition may be hard-wired into us, in a healthy artistic environment, artists are not in competition with each other. Unfortunately, healthy artistic

environments are about as common as unicorns.
We live in a society that encourages competition
at demonstrably vicious levels.

—*David Bayles and Ted Orland in their book,* Art & Fear

THE INNER CRITIC: WHERE DOES IT COME FROM?

Talking with a psychologist friend about the eternal presence, in our psyches, of the inner critic, provided an insight. She reminded me that the inner critic is linked with the superego, the part of our personality that contains moral values and principles that allow us to live relatively safely in society. So this voice is necessary, just often dysfunctional when it interferes with our creative work. Yet, with time and courage, we manage to find and free our authentic artist selves.

I found that my own inner critic had roots in my mother's fearful voice. I can still hear the exact words she said to me when I was in my early 30s. We were having an intense argument about my life choices; I was working in non-profit theatre, teaching a couple of daytime classes and teaching or rehearsing two to four evenings a week, and going out to perform on weekend nights. When I was working, my son, about three at the time, was either in preschool or day care or home with his dad in the evenings. I was with my boy more than many mothers with full-time jobs. But I wasn't earning a decent living. My income was very modest (a situation I did not enjoy), and from my mother's perspective, I should have a "real job" or stay home with my kid. In the heat of anger, she said, "You overestimate your talent." The words felt like a knife to the gut. As many artists do, I often worried about having "enough talent." She couldn't have said anything more damning. I know now that she was worried about my material security and trying, in her way, to keep me safe. In the therapy sessions I mentioned above, I've had many conversations with my invisible mother and played my mother talking with me.

Here's another example of an inner critic that originated in an outward one. Harry, a student of mine, who is required by his job to make frequent public presentations, had been giving speeches for a couple of years with little difficulty, often enjoying the task. He believed in the value of the message he was delivering and wanted others to have this information.

Then his boss got him a coach, who would be backstage with Harry, telling him to make sure he stood in the right place, used the microphone a particular way, controlled his gestures to look the way the coach thought they should look and modulated his voice just so. That's when Harry's performance anxiety began. Instead of focusing on the meaning of the material and his connection with his listeners, he found himself judging his delivery against the "right" and "wrong" standards of the coach. Spontaneity left him. The task of speaking became onerous. He came to improvisation class to recover his spontaneity, and over time, he did. He convinced his boss that he didn't need the coach and eventually found his way back to more ease in his presentations.

SOME SUGGESTIONS TO COUNTER STAGE FRIGHT

- In the main, the audience will be as engaged as we are. If we are fully committed to what we are doing on stage (or on the "stage" of life) we will care more about what we are doing than about what other people think. Our habitual concern, voiced by our inner critic, "They'll find me boring" or "What if they hate my content or style?" is the primary obstacle to our creativity. If we can locate the original source of this nagging voice, we can begin to find some freedom from its impact. We can have a dialogue with this voice and counter its hostile messages. You will find help with this process in the book: Embracing Your Inner Critic, mentioned earlier.

- Psychotherapy can help. In addition to my phobia therapy, I've spent many fruitful (and sometimes frustrating) hours with a variety of therapists. My favorite forms being Gestalt and drama therapy; both involve role-playing and interaction with the therapist. Hypnosis is often effective at uncovering, and helping to heal, past sources of emotional trauma. Though I've never tried it, I've known actors (and non-actors) who've used EMDR (eye movement desensitization and reprogramming) with a therapist, and found a reduction in anxiety.

- We can develop soothing pre-show rituals that can relax us. Include sensory awareness, deep breathing, and a warm-up that combines movement and some encouraging self-talk, such as: "I'm ready to join with my partners to create a great show," "I'm happy to be here doing what I love." "I'm really going to enjoy this show" (or speech or presentation). Or "My mind is clear and my heart is open." All phrases I've used. Create your own statements that are true for you. In recent years, when I found myself performing less often, I would often say to myself, "I'm so grateful that I get to perform tonight." If you don't believe the self-talk, it probably won't help. You can't fool the psyche. You may need to talk about your feelings with your colleagues.

- Another simple and collaborative palliative for anxiety is HUGGING. Yeah, there's research on that. It works. In my troupe, we'd often give each other brief back and shoulder rubs. Touch is so reassuring and connecting.

- Some people pray or chant before a show, some do yoga, some meditate and some carry a good luck talisman. Some, to relax and open the heart, watch comic movies or videos of their adorable kids. (I've been known to watch one-minute grandson videos.)

- I find it useful to visualize myself on stage enjoying being there and giving the performance I want to create. Also, I conjure up a sense memory of a past time when I was relaxed and happy on stage—or off. Get in touch with your original need to express yourself: to share something you love.

- Our anxiety triggers a flood of adrenaline into our system, getting us ready for "fight or flight." Movement can flush some of the adrenaline out, restoring more psychophysical balance. Backstage, if you have the space, dance, shake, run in place, stretch. Take classes to learn these techniques. I never perform without warming up. Check the exercises Singing Yawn, Baby Rolls and other warm-up techniques. One improvisation colleague of mine would often leave the theatre a half hour before curtain and jog around the block. Sometimes, when it felt right, I'd join her. Social psychologist Amy Cuddy suggests that "power posing," assuming a powerful-looking physical pose (which she calls the Wonder Woman pose) for two minutes, can make you feel more powerful and confident. All of these activities will tend to ground your consciousness in your body, which is just where it needs to be.

- Some performers take beta-blockers, a class of prescription drugs, to help calm them. Some take a stiff drink or smoke some pot. Both of these strategies have their obvious risks— and they don't address the underlying issues triggering the anxiety.

- I once heard Jerry Seinfeld in an interview say that he "can't do accents." That didn't keep him from being wildly successful at what he DOES do well. Focus on what you're good at, not on what you're not good at. Of course you want to face what is difficult for you and expand your range of skills but you don't need to be good at everything.

- Get back on the boards as soon as you can after an unpleasant performance experience, perhaps in a less intimidating context; a class or practice with friends. As in all activities, the more you practice, the more skill you develop and with skill comes more ease. Still, most of the students I've taught and many of my professional colleagues, including myself, have suffered from some degree of stage fright at some point in our lives. I read an interview with dancer Mikhail

Baryshnikov, a virtuoso in his form, who said that he experiences stage fright before almost every show but once he's into the performance, he enjoys it. He's not the only famous performer who has struggled with the beast of fear. There's also Sir Lawrence Olivier and Barbara Streisand and many others. There will be failures, that's certain. I've survived many of them and I'm still on my feet. You have to choose, over and over, to do the work. Or not.

TALENT

> *Talent is nothing but a prolonged period of attention*
> *and a shortened period of mental assimilation.*
>
> —*Constantin Stanislavski*

What is talent? One dictionary definition says it's "a natural ability or aptitude…" We know that all people have the capacity to be creative, but everyone is not creative in the same way. Some may have a gift for science, for invention, for visual art or design, for music, for healing others. Perhaps talent in the arts is a passionate and sensitive temperament joined with a strong need for creative expression. As we've observed, dramatic play is an intrinsic part of human development. All healthy children have unfettered imaginations. Therefore, an essential part of improvisational theatre training is a journey to recover and develop a natural facility that has been lost through socialization.

I've worked with people for whom the work came easily: extroverted, quick, lots of stage presence, flexible body, with easy access to the unconscious. And I've worked with many people who've had to struggle with shyness, with a fierce inner critic, with a stiff body. I've found that the person who can commit himself to the learning process, weathering the obstacles, can evolve into a skilled and unique performer, whom people will see as talented. Improvisation is a skill like any other, and skills can be learned. The old saw,

"It's 10 percent inspiration and 90 percent perspiration," seems to be accurate. The process of skill development over time can be very satisfying and liberating in itself. If the learner commits to the journey, she can relax through the rocky as well as the smooth periods with the sense of onward progression ever present.

It's not constructive to worry about whether or not we have talent. The real questions are: Have I found a form of self-expression that I love? Am I willing to do the work? Am I willing to "get back on the horse" when I fail?

TUNING THE INSTRUMENT: TRAINING THE BODY, THE VOICE AND THE IMAGINATION

Movement is the stuff of great communication.

—*Agnes de Mille*

he exercises that form the core of FSI workshops are listed in this chapter. Some will be familiar to comedy improv students, some to students of movement theatre and drama therapy and some to trained actors. These are in the canon because they are as essential to learning the fundmentals of improvisational theatre as scales are to learning music. Some very popular exercises are carefully explained in many other books, so in these cases I may mention the exercise and refer the reader to another source for details. I'll describe in detail my favorite well-known exercises and the less familiar techniques, some of which I've reinterpreted from another teacher, some of which I've made up. Most exercises practice and integrate several skills at once: movement and sound; relaxation, concentration and connection; language and timing, and so on. Heightened awareness of self, others, and environment (mindfulness) is basic to all aspects of this work. You can do the same exercises again and again and they will always give you something different back.

CHECKING IN

So, dear reader, since sensory awareness is at the core of this work, I suggest that, as soon as you finish reading this paragraph, you take a small break to check in to yourself: body/mind/emotions/spirit—and ask yourself what you're feeling and needing right now:

- To get up and stretch?
- Or go out for walk?
- To make a cup of tea?
- To meditate?
- To phone your sister?

- To sing or dance?
- Or take a nap?
- What's going on in your body?
- What images or thoughts are foremost in your mind?
- Would you like to write in your journal?
- Start a journal?

I encourage you to take this creativity/self-care break whenever you have the opportunity.

Here we go, on to the exercises.

Though I have strong aesthetic preferences about improvisational theatre and cherished beliefs about effective teaching, the techniques and exercises offered here are not sacrosanct. I encourage you to use them as jumping-off places from which you can discover your own creative journey.

Some exercises are transcribed almost verbatim from in-class sessions. Some I sat and wrote down. I like the "live action" lessons because they reveal something about teaching style. I did edit out some of the repetition in instructions, but I strongly support using repetition in teaching, as it's essential to learning. Example: When people are moving about the studio in ensemble locomotion, I remind them over and over to let their eyes be at eye level, which allows the head to be on top of the spine, so the skeleton can be in alignment. It also allows actors to be available to their partners through eye contact. In the public world, we're used to looking down at the sidewalk, for safety, and when we're thinking we often look down. It's an entrenched habit that won't be broken by a single instruction.

WARM-UPS

To prepare the psychophysical self for creative activity we use exercises that move the body, voice, and psyche into a state of relaxed readiness. The effect is to:

- Expand sensory awareness

- Open and energize the body and voice

- Prepare ourselves to respond intuitively to stimuli from outside and impulse from within

Many, not all, group warm-ups are done in a circle. The group makes a lovely circle with the distance from their colleagues on the right and on the left the same. This is the beginning of awareness of space, noticing how the beauty of a conscious shape can support centering and concentration and can be aesthetically satisfying. When standing in the circle for a length of time I often suggest, between exercises, that the students move to a new place in the circle, with different people on each side.

Following are detailed warm-up suggestions. Use all or part of any of them, depending on how much focus and time you want to devote to in-depth work with the body/mind. Some you can do alone, some with a partner or a group.

ON THE MAT

Melt down into your mat and just take a moment to stretch out on your back. Relax and release, letting your weight sink into the mat. Take a moment to check into your body with a sensory body scan. Let your awareness move through your body from head to toe and toe to head. Where, in your body, are you released? Where held? Where warm? Where cool? (You can find even more detailed sensory awareness exercises on the Internet).

Really notice the changes in your body and thoughts from moment to moment. Focusing on the breath, notice that the exhalation is the release breath, the relaxation phase of breathing. The inhalation is more of an energizing breath. There are actually three parts to your breathing: the in, the out and the pause before the new breath. You can let this pause be as long as it wants to be and the vacuum action of the lungs will draw in the new breath. This can be deeply relaxing and centering.

- We'll work through a progression of movements from lying down:

Move into a long stretch on your back, arms above the head, back of the hands on the floor. Let your legs be extended and flex through your ankles, stretch out from the center, tilt the back of your waist and rib cage into the floor, pushing the stomach muscles towards the floor eliminating the natural arch in your back. Breathe. Now let it go and hug your knees to your chest. Do this a couple of times (more if you like) then try this meditative movement:

MEDITATIVE MOVEMENT

On your back with eyes closed, arms still over your head, stretched out, begin very slowly to lift both arms together up in the air making an arc on either side of your body as the arms move from above your head to the mat near your thighs. Control the speed of the movement to keep the arms at a constant pace. Do this as slowly as you can and you'll feel how gravity works on your muscles. Exhale on the lifting movement. After several arcs up and down, play with the tempo a little. Then try the arm movement opening to each side with arms floating up from the mat to above the center of your chest where your palms can meet in a prayer-like pose. Then, at some point, you can play with the range of motion of your arms when on your back. Knowing this movement has a ritual quality helps you decide when to do it. It works well to do before toning or chanting.

Now, keep moving in a way that is very slow and continuous. Let a part of your body always be in motion. Either the whole body can be in motion, or one part can be in motion and then another can pick it up. Don't worry about trying to get it right. It's really about how you drop into the direct experience of physicality, the sensation: the sense of heat on the skin, the sense of energy that's moving through you, the sense of motion through space.

MOVING FOR THE PLEASURE OF IT

Move through a short series of stretches from the yoga sun salute and/or other yoga moves. Take a few minutes to complete your warm-up. Checking into your body, what does it need at this moment? Make modifications for your own physical limitations. Do what you can. Take the attitude of "moving for the pleasure of it." Pick and chose movements to meet the particular needs of any particular day. Then, to get up, while engaging the voice, try this:

UP AND DOWN THREE WAYS

From lying on your back, start to move towards standing up. Take your time. Make your way from lying down, all the way up to standing and back down to lying again, three times, going through all the levels. Get up and down in a different way every time. Also, start to vocalize as you move; humming, singing, talking to yourself, mumbling, just so you are using your voice as you get up and get down three times, feeling the voice as part of the body. The soundtrack to this exercise is any sound you allow yourself to make. You're still focusing on sensation, kinesthetic awareness. You're sensing the body from the inside. Moving slowly or quickly between levels, noticing what happens as you change levels. (If this is a problem, if it's difficult to get up and down, maybe get up and down only once, slowly.) The third time you find yourself standing, stay there.

Now, standing, imagine your head floating off the top of the spine, just floating like a helium balloon. Your spine is growing longer, like a monkey's tail. Envision your central vertical axis like a plum line dropping through your body, a silk string connecting you to the heavens and the earth. These are images that will affect the nervous system and stimulate the imagination.

Take a moment to look around, see where you are, check into how you feel and see whom you are with.

If you've got adrenaline rushing through your system, try shaking your body. Standing, with knees and all joints loose, start with a tiny stomping of your feet and let the shake move upward through the whole body. Accompany this movement with a breathy Haaa or Huh sound every couple of exhalations.

BABY ROLL

Do this very comforting movement after mat relaxation and stretching. Lie on your back with legs extended, arms at sides. Draw legs up, folding your knees to your chest, with elbows bent, open hands, letting palms be facing up near your shoulders. Begin to let your whole torso roll back and forth. Let the torso roll all the way to the right, then to the left. The head rolls back and forth on the mat. Let your hand be on the floor in front of your face or near your face as your cheek is close to the mat. You're going to be able to push with that hand so you roll to the other side, a little push, back and forth on a rounded spine and with this try a little "haaaa" sound as you roll. Can you love rolling around on a floor; can you remember what it was to be a delighted baby? Then let the momentum of the roll and the hand push take you up to sitting and back down again. In sitting, one leg will be folded in front of you, one leg folded to the side. When you're ready, roll back to the center and let it go.

Then drop your feet to the floor, stretch out your legs, stretch out your arms above your head, a long stretch out from the center, and tilt the lower back and the back of the waist into the mat, lengthening. Using your stomach muscles, you eliminate that natural arch in your lower back. Flex through your heels as you do that and push your elbows towards the floor. Big stretch. Flatten towards the mat, then exhale and hug your knees, and inhale as you open. Repeat, exhale, and try to bring your head up towards your knees when you're doing this curly one. Then drop your feet to the mat, and relax.

Now a couple of pelvic tilts: pushing your feet into the mat while tilting the tailbone up towards the ceiling. Coming down from the top, one vertebra at a time, slowly. Try getting a new breath when your pelvis is up, releasing the breath while moving down.

> Notice how the imagination is fueled by sensation. What images or thoughts are arising? There may be content material here. The body is constantly informing the imagination, which is different from having an idea and trying to find the body for it. How do they interact with each other? In reality you can't take them apart: ideas and images create feeling state, sensation triggers memories. As the thoughts float in and out of your mind, keep bringing your focus back to your body.

Here's another version of an aware warm-up adapted from the book, *An Acrobat of the Heart* by Stephen Wangh.

STREAM-OF-CONSCIOUSNESS WARM-UP

During your warm-up, to help you notice what's happening, try mumbling your thoughts out loud. Sometimes you will find that you are thinking about what your body is doing, but at other moments you may notice that you're thinking about other things. Perhaps you are noticing the space or the people around you, or you are daydreaming or judging your work. In any case, don't try to stop your mind from wandering.

Then try this: every time your mind enters a new thought or feeling, purposefully change what you are doing with your body. The important thing is to notice the changes in your inner world, and to mark those changes by changing your activity. You want to make your outward choices reflect your inner states. For instance, if your mind is racing about nervously, you might literally race around the room. If you feel angry and frustrated, you might kick or punch the air. If you are feeling lost, you might crawl into a corner. You don't have to find exactly the right thing to do; just let your body somehow reflect the mind's activity. See if each time a new thought enters your mind you can change what you're doing and do something new, something that allows your whole body to reflect the new emotion or mental activity. Continue to work this way until the process of noticing changes is clear to you, at least six or seven minutes. You may find yourself at times forgetting to notice your thoughts. This may mean that you are completely focused on the sensations in your body. That's lovely; enjoy it. You will likely come back to your thoughts. Now take a minute with your eyes closed to let yourself reflect on what you have gone through, and how you feel now. Remember what happened. How does the condition of your body and of your mind now compare with their condition before you started this warm-up? How do they compare with how they feel after your usual warm-up?

LION'S ROAR

Lion's Roar is a fun move with sound to do before you come to standing. On mats with yoga lion stretch, fold back into the yoga Child's Pose and spring forward with a growl or roar—Very freeing and enlivening. Good to do before you work with animal images for character.

SENSORY AWARENESS

Standing, notice how your feet feel on the floor. We'll put the feet in an aligned position, under the knees, and the knees under the thigh sockets. Joints are lined up. Without looking down at your feet, make the two inner lines of your feet, parallel. Then, look at your feet and see if they are, in fact, parallel. For many people, your sensory awareness is not accurate, so what you feel the body is doing is not necessarily what it is doing. This will often show itself in performance, with actors thinking they're doing very big, bold gestures or movements or using their voice loudly, when in fact their behavior is subtle or understated. For learning about body and voice habits and self-perception, video is an effective, though difficult, teacher. After seeing themselves on video, many students see the difference between what they felt and how it was actually manifested physically. I use video as a learning tool for performing students and warn them to expect harsh judgment from their inner critic, until they get used to the often unflattering nature of video and learn to use it gently.

HELP EACH OTHER UP

In pairs, one person is lying down and the other helps him to stand up. Negotiate how much weight can be given to the lifter, so that the action is safe and effective for both bodies. Try lifting two or three different ways, then switch roles.

SINGING YAWN

The singing yawn is just that: releasing sound while yawning, waking up the breath and the voice. Let the breath drop down to the bowl of the pelvis, drop your jaw open and yawn as fully as you can while releasing big vowel sounds.

You want a real yawn because your throat is very open during a yawn and you're inhaling generous amounts of air. If you're not getting a real yawn try this: let the jaw drop wide and quickly breathe in a big swallow of air through your mouth into the back of your throat, near your palate. Once you've released a yawn, you may find yourself needing to yawn more during the next hour or so. Please do not inhibit yawning in class. It's a release of tension and fills your lungs with air. Let it be full and deep. This is a fundamental voice warm-up.

(Yawning without covering the mouth is the first taboo we break in class. It triggers embarrassment in some new students which I tell them is fine. No one ever died of embarrassment. By class number two, the embarrassment is gone. Activities that we do regularly begin to feel "normal" after a while.)

Next, stretch the face (a primary revealer of emotion) and give yourself a little face massage. Then stick out your tongue as long and as far as possible and rotate it one direction for 3 or 4 licks, and then reverse. The lips, tongue and teeth are the articulators for speech.

Kick and Hoots

HORSE'S LIPS

Flutter your pursed lips by blowing through them, making a sound. Then add shaking the body loose, like a rag doll or over-cooked pasta and trotting around the space with loose body, doing the horse's lips. After 30 seconds or so add the sounds "yum, yum, yum," interspersed with horse's lips.

LINKED MOVEMENT

Next is a good practice, taken from Contact Improvisation, to follow helping each other up. It's a trust exercise as well as a work-out. The actors stand, face to face, about three feet apart and clasp each other's wrists as they lean away from each other, letting their balance become interdependent. Elbows should remain open, not bent. They explore what movement can happen while connected: lowering bodies slowly into a squat and back up, crossing arms, releasing one arm from its grasp while moving down and up.... Then try back-to-back, interdependently leaning into each other, going up and down to a squat and back to standing.

KICKS AND HOOTS

In the circle, all make a percussive hooting sound. The sound resonates in the pallet, high in the back of the throat. We add sharp kicks into the center of the circle and energize the space by opening and closing our hands. We'll expand and contract the circle, moving in unison, rhythmically, following the leader, hooting, kicking and throwing energy out through our hands into the center of the circle.

IMAGE WALKS

Begin walking around the studio noticing how you feel today. Let go of any tensions you have and just walk. When an image is called out, respond immediately in any way that comes to you, allowing the image to work on you. Then, when the leader says, "Let it go," shake out your body and return to walking.

> The floor is covered two feet deep in feathers.
>
> The floor is covered with ice.
>
> The floor is three feet deep in mud.
>
> The floor is covered with hot coals.
>
> The floor is very sticky.
>
> The floor is water and sand like in the shallows of the ocean.
>
> The air is full of balloons.
>
> There are bullets flying three feet above the ground.
>
> There are nude people lying on the floor.

MORE MOVEMENT IDEAS / IMAGES FOR WARM-UP

> Collapsing or melting into the floor as an ice cream cone on a hot day.
>
> Working your way down against resistance.

Jumping up, surprising yourself to standing as a Jack-in-the-Box.

Feeling the feet rooted like a tree, imagining wind blowing the tree about.

Dancing to rhythm/music in a staccato way or chaotic or lyrical or slow motion or expansive movement, or released or contracted/held movement.

MARIONETTES

Individuals in circle: Think of yourself as a marionette with a big puppeteer up in the sky who is moving your limbs. Imagine strings on your hands and wrists. What are the possibilities of movement? (Practice for 2 minutes or so.) Now add strings to your elbows and knees and feet. Explore moving around with that imagery for a few minutes. Now, imagine somebody cutting the strings for each of those places. You have the control of your body back.

You may want to add Grotowski Plastiques to your warm-up. They are rich physical/emotional movements, explained in great detail in Stephen Wangh's book, *An Acrobat of The Heart*, and in Grotowski's own book, *Towards a Poor Theatre*. They take time to learn but are worth exploring.

PAIR AND ENSEMBLE EXERCISES

It is sometimes thought that in Improvisation we can do just anything. But lack of a conscious plan does not mean that our work is random or arbitrary. When we are totally faithful to our own individuality we are actually following a very intricate design. This kind of freedom is the opposite of "just anything."

—*Stephen Nachmanovitch,* Free Play, Improvisation in Life and Art

I learned many variations of ensemble movement structures from Anna Halprin, John Graham and Mary Overlie. You can also find lots more in *The Viewpoints Book* by Anne Bogart and Tina Landau. Try experimenting with ensemble movement and you'll discover many possibilities yourself.

SENDING AND RECEIVING

LEADER / FOLLOWER
Pairs

I always do this exercise early on in the beginner classes as leading and following are fundamental elements of improvisation and of any relationship. We are practicing moving together with ease.

In pairs, standing at your partner's side, shoulder to shoulder, take a moment to close your eyes, feel your feet on the floor, relax, and let your breath drop down to the bottom of the pelvic bowl. Notice your breathing. Then, with your eyes closed, start sensing your partner next to you and let yourself notice your partner's breath. So, it's a loop of energy, sending and receiving messages between you and your partner. (Take 10-15 seconds or so.) This is a simple exercise. When you are the leader, you're going to take your partner for a walk around the space. As you're traveling together you'll make the decisions about where you're going and how you're moving. If you're the follower, you'll just enjoy going along for the ride.

Before you begin moving, connect physically in some way that is comfortable for you to walk together linked: hand on the shoulder, hand on the back of the waist, linking arms, holding hands, any way. Decide who is the first leader: A is apple, that's the leader. You're going to switch later. If you're B, if you're banana, you're the follower. So, Apple, go ahead and take your partner for a walk. Begin to move around the space together, eyes open for everybody. Do this without speaking. Let your eyes be in soft focus. All eyes are at eye-level, so you're seeing where you're going. Notice, when you're looking straight ahead, how you can see a lot with your peripheral vision, a lot of information coming in.

Put your focus on your physical connection with your partner. If you're not comfortable with the way you're holding each other, change. Now, the point of this exercise is to move together with ease. So if you're pulling your partner about, you need to slow down and simplify. And if you're the follower, check and see: Are you resisting? Could you give up that resistance? Could you enjoy being a follower for a little bit? Might be quite relaxing, joining in with your partner (side coach as the actors move): Ahhh, everybody release your breath, let your hands be free, keep going, keep moving forward, all eyes at eye level, not on the floor.

Apples, you want to have a destination, take your partner someplace, move through the space with intention. (They've been moving for 3-4 minutes) Now, if it's becoming very easy to move with your partner, then go ahead and add something more complicated, like trotting, skipping, stopping and starting, going backwards. If you are walking backwards, you need to have the eyes in the back of your head open, and your sonar on. Now keep going without a break and let the other person lead. A is now B and B is A. Just slide into it. Try a new way of holding each other: maybe back of the waist, shoulder, whatever. Change your point of contact frequently. Moving together with ease, that's the objective. Breathe, everybody, exhale! Don't hold your breath! And again, there's the principle of moving for the pleasure of it.

If it gets awkward, if your partner is not with you, go back to simple. Change leaders again: let the other person lead. Signaling through the body, not talking. You're not giving your partner dance lessons, you are just moving together with ease. That's all. This is a collaboration. Can you give up trying to get your partner to do what you want? Can you let go of that and see if you can find something that is pleasant and easy for both of you. Switch leadership again. Good. Is it getting easier, smoother? (After 2-3 more minutes.)

Now, I won't tell you when to switch. You are both leading and both following. Sometimes, you're going to take the leadership and sometimes your partner is going to take it, without anyone saying. Be ready to pick up the leadership, be ready to let it go. See if you can enjoy being a leader and enjoy being a follower. Pass it back and forth. Sometimes it's a smooth transition, some-

times not so smooth, and sometimes you are just moving to the same drummer. You might not even quite know who is leading, a lovely feeling of collaboration. (Side-coach the actors to notice the differences that occur in their psychophysical tensions when they go from leader to follower or vice versa.)

Now one person is a free card and she is going to connect with anybody she wants, so sometimes you'll have a threesome and the person in the middle will lead. Now you're in touch with two people. Notice how that feels different. Like all exercises, this will get easier with practice and with relaxing into it.

In ten seconds let your partner go, say farewell without words. (I count to 10 out loud, softly, and then say, "Release") Now move through the space on your own in the way your body wants to move. Release and enjoy. As you move, let your eyes be at eye level and make eye contact with the people you are passing. Eventually you'll connect with someone and that will be your new partner. Play with her. One of you will lead initially and then you'll pass the leadership back and forth. After a few minutes leave your partner and pick up a new one whenever the desire strikes. Do what feels good when you're on your own for a few seconds or a minute. We'll change partners two or three times.

After this exercise, in a beginner class, I'll ask people to notice if they were more comfortable being a leader or being a follower. I suggest that we need to enjoy and embrace both roles. We often debrief, having a short discussion.

TELL ME ABOUT YOURSELF
Pairs

Now, with a new partner, we'll continue Leader/Follower and add verbal life. One of you is the questioner and one is the talker. Again, A and B. The questioner has a very limited script. All you can say is: "Tell me about yourself, please," "thank you," and your partner's name. You may use those words in any order, as often as needed, to get your partner to speak. If she is already speaking continuously you just listen. Can you stay present in the movement as you speak?

This exercise can be followed by a simple performance (good for beginners) in which each player takes a turn introducing their partner to the group using the information they've just heard. If you tell the students ahead of time that they'll introduce their partners later, they'll listen more attentively. It's also enlightening to have the students do a short round of "Tell Me About Yourself" without telling them that they need to remember what they're hearing and then have them introduce their partners. Then have them repeat the exercise, knowing that they'll be introducing and see how much more they remember. You can remind actors to notice what they are thinking, as they are listening. Often we're thinking about what we want to say, instead of simply listening.

SELF–INTRO THREE DIFFERENT WAYS, IN THE CIRCLE
Beginner/Intermediate

As a way of introducing ourselves, we'll go around and have every person say her or his name with a movement. And then the whole group will reflect it back. You'll do it twice: once by yourself and once with the whole ensemble, all in unison.

First, just do this for the pleasure of self-expression. Try not to rehearse it in your mind; when it's your turn just go with your impulse.

- After everyone has done this once, we'll go around the circle again. This time say your name with a movement or gesture that reveals a part of yourself about which you feel critical, that you usually like to hide. A couple of words or a phrase may be added in addition to your name.

- Third time: show us the persona that you like to present to the world, how you like to be seen.

(These self-revelatory actions are the most endowed with feeling and are often powerful, surprising, and funny. This may be repeated as most people have a long list of self-judgments.)

MOVING IN A CIRCLE

All improvisers are walking in a circle, rhythm unified, and following each other. They keep the distance between the person in front and the one in back even and constant. The teacher will change the tempo of the walking and all will notice and join the new tempo as quickly as possible. Then one player in the group will do that, then another. Players may also add movement changes such as skipping, trotting, extending arms, adding sound. All will join the action. Here's a variation:

When the leader says, "Turn," movers pivot around in unison and switch directions. When the leader says, "Break circle," they release from the circle and move about the space in individual ways until the leader says, "Form circle," at which time they recreate the circle as quickly as possible and move together again.

- All move in straight lines.
- All move in only curved lines.
- The leadership can be passed around. Actors are practicing moving back and forth between individual impulse and ensemble unity.
- Add emotional charge:

While moving in ensemble around the studio, improvisers endow one person in the group with the identity of someone to whom they are attracted and another person who scares or repulses them. Then try changing these endowments. This is fiction. It's not your actual classmate. See how this effects how and where you move.

> *You can discover more about a person in an hour of play than in a year of conversation.*
>
> —*Plato*

SOUND BALL

Making eye contact and using gesture and voice, throw the sound, as though it were a ball, to someone else in the circle. The receiver catches the ball with the same sound that was sent and then transforms that sound and gesture and sends a new one to another player across the circle.

WORD BALL

Simple verbal-life warm-up, using free association. Again, making eye contact and using gesture, throw the imaginary ball accompanied by a word. Receiver responds with a new word as he throws.

IMAGE BALL

Same game, but this time players speak a phrase or sentence that describes something: "Bright sun streaming in through the window." "The blond toddler was screaming at the top of his lungs." "In the room, the atmosphere was tense." Receivers respond on impulse, given no time to think, saying any phrase that comes to them. They need not "make sense." In early training, students often feel they are "wrong" if their offers are not logical or linear. Relieving them of this responsibility tends to free the imagination.

GESTURE CIRCLE

Standing in the circle, one person at a time offers a gesture that is either very big and intense or very small and subtle. It may, or may not, include sound. The gesture will be passed around the circle. If it is small, each new player will expand it incrementally so that by the time it gets around the whole circle, it's big and intense. If it is large, it will become smaller and subtler. The emotional color of the movement should be clear throughout. Notice if your gesture includes waving—what images does that trigger? If it includes covering your face, what image emerges?

If you look into the distance or over your shoulder, how does that affect your emotional life?

To be clear, a gesture usually involves the limbs, head and possibly the torso and is done in place, as contrasted to whole body movement, such as running, jumping, collapsing. You can use the gestures created in the circle to begin scenes or include in scenes you do later in class or in practice.

ROLPHING
Beginners

Done in the circle, this process is sometimes referred to as "vomiting words," and consists of starting with a sound (such as eeaah) as opposed to a full word. Once the sound is projected, the actor must come up with a word related to the sound, or a word that includes the sound, often surprising even the speaker himself. You can also let several words emerge from one sound, creating phrases.

MOVEMENT/SOUND REFLECTING CIRCLE. This popular exercise practices spontaneity and gets people to move and sound in unaccustomed ways, as they mirror their partner's offers. It's very simple. Essentially it's just passing the impulses around the circle. One person will start with offering a sound and movement to the person next to you. Then the receiver is going to reflect the action back as accurately as she can. Then she's going to repeat that received action until it transforms to a new one and she'll offer the new movement and sound to her neighbor on the other side, who will reflect it back and then find a new action to pass on, etc.

Notice if you're pausing to think after you've reflected back your neighbor's offer. See if you can skip that thinking phase. Let the body do it, not the mind.

See if you can just let the first move morph into the next. Keep the action and energy moving around the circle.

MOVEMENT/SOUND STIMULUS/RESPONSE CIRCLE. This has the same structure as Reflecting Circle. But the action is different. Instead of reflecting your neighbor's offer, you will respond to the offer with an action that embodies your immediate feelings. Notice what your body/mind really wants to do when you receive the offer. If the offer is a shout with your partner moving towards you, do you want to shout back or to run away or to laugh at your partner…? What do you want to do? Let yourself enact your impulse, then as you turn to the next person in the circle, your action will transform into a new one. (In a beginner class, after the students have gone around the circle a couple of times, the leader may want to point out that they have just performed a very small, mini scene, as stimulus/response is the fundamental action of a scene.)

HANDSHAKES AND GREETINGS
Beginner/Intermediate

This is a playful warm-up, stimulating the imagination, a "getting to know each other game," to be done with a new group.

Move about the space in your own tempo, awakening your spatial awareness and sense of ensemble (being part of the whole). At the teacher's signal introduce yourself to someone you're passing by extending your hand for a handshake and saying "Hi (or hello), I'm so and so." At first speak English and use your real name. Keep milling about and connecting with each other as you pass. Next, at the teacher's signal let the name you call yourself be in a foreign language or make it up on the spot. Then use any name except your own. For example: "Hi, I'm Travis (for a woman)," or "Hello, I'm Dr. Feelgood." While shaking hands your partner will answer back "Good to meet you Doctor (or some such thing), I'm Mrs. Blankenship."

Then move on quickly to the next person and introduce yourself again using a different name. Keep milling about, encountering new players. Keep this up for a while until the teacher tells you to use a name of a thing as your own name: "My name is Buzzsaw" or Mashed Potatoes or Flowing Water, whatever comes to mind, feeling for a name that might reveal something about who you are at the moment. Also, feel free to add a phrase such as "I'm new here," "Glad to meet you"—"You make me hungry"—any response to your partner's verbal offer. This game could be a lead in to Leader/Follower or any ensemble movement and sound exercise.

HAND DANCE / FEET DANCE

In pairs, standing, students are spread throughout the studio. They're going to have a "conversation" using only their hands and lower arms. They'll be silent and focus their eyes on each other's hands. Tell them to explore how much feeling and information they can convey within this constraint. They are free to keep standing or to sit or to get up and down, as needed. They may travel a little. They may touch but are not to rely on touch exclusively.

One day, doing this exercise this question was asked:

Student: Should we avoid giving the finger or making our hands like a gun?

Joya: It's not my policy to forbid any creative impulse (except dangerous or hurtful ones) but I think you already know how to do those things. How about exploring unfamiliar shapes and gestures?"

The Feet Dance has basically the same structure, but players are sitting on the floor or chairs "speaking" with their feet and ankles only. Most of the time they are to avoid looking at each other's faces.

GROUP MACHINE, GROUP ANIMAL

Best done with 5-8 improvisers. This practices ensemble collaboration and visual imagery. Players are warmed up and ready for movement. The first mover creates a repeated movement and sound phrase that invokes the qualities of a machine: sharp, percussive, mechanical. Player #2 joins in, moving very close to #1, adding his moves/sounds in response to #1. Each subsequent player adds another part with the intention of building a continuously moving machine, making a moving sculpture, while paying attention to sound possibilities.

The same process can be followed with round, sensual movement and animal sounds to create a fantasy animal made up of actors' bodies moving together.

To dismantle the machine or animal, you can try actors leaving the group, one at a time, in reverse order, starting with actor number one. You can also explore the forming and dismantling of the entities, with players leaving in random order or the whole thing collapsing or exploding or morphing into something else.

GROUP GO, A CONCENTRATION AND CONNECTION GAME
Beginner / Intermediate

In the circle

Narration of this exercise from class:

Let your chest be open with a sense of being receptive. Now look around the circle and see who's with you in the room. See if you know everybody's name. Who knows all the names? Would you name everyone for us? (Student names people) If you just know 4 or 5 names for this game, it will work. You don't have to know everybody's name. By the end of the game you will.

Look around the circle and make eye contact with somebody. I see Tina right across the circle from me and we're making eye contact. So I'm going to look at her and I'm going to say her name, Tina. And by saying that, I'm asking for her spot. I want to be where she is. So she's going to say, "Go," and that means I can move across the circle and take her place. Now in order to vacate her spot for me, she needs a place to go, so she makes eye contact with another player, maybe Jonathan, and after she says his name he will say, "Go," so she can have his spot. And then Jonathan has to look at and name somebody, Annie, and she says, "Go." You cannot leave your place until someone says, "Go" to you.

This is about a couple of things. It's about concentration and about being available to be contacted, being present in the room with each other. So, if you drop your eyes down you're going to lose the action. If your mind goes out of the room, you'll notice it because you'll probably lose the flow. You need all your attention here at this moment. It's a simple game, but profound in terms of concentration.

Okay, Tina, say "Go." (She says "Go.") Now you have to find a spot to move to. And everybody, you can be ornery and not say go when asked, but then the game just stops and nothing happens. So, I ask you to just say "Go" and be ready to give up your spot. Tina, find a place to go. Look at somebody and ask for their spot. (A student misses her cue and stutters trying to remember a name.) Now, I want to point something out. We're laughing, right? Because comedy is based on foibles, based on human mistakes. It's not based on perfection. You laugh when somebody messes up.

Is anyone getting uptight with this exercise? Are you worried about doing it right? You will do it wrong and nothing will happen to you. I won't fire you or give you a bad grade. So that's the thing, concentration works better when you relax. You can mess up; it's ok. Look around again and see who's here. It doesn't matter how fast this game goes. It's not about speed. It's about connection and presence. Just take your time. Eye contact is essential in this, as you'll see in the next part of the game.

The next level goes like this: If you want Rebecca's spot, instead of saying "Rebecca," you'll make it clear to her through eye contact and gesture that you want her spot. When she says "Go" you move. No more names are spoken. If you don't have your eyes available, it isn't going to work.

In Part Three, all your communication is done silently. You'll make it clear through your behavior that you're giving up your spot or that you want someone's spot. You'll make eye contact and use gesture. (The atmosphere of concentration is intense at this point.) Ah, yes, see how smoothly this is going now. (Students usually report that this part of the game is the most enjoyable.)

TRUST FALLS

Yes, this is a touchy-feely game from the 1960s. It still does the trick: practices risk-taking, trust, and collaboration.

Form groups of 5 to 7. One person falls, the others catch. The group arranges itself in two equal parallel lines, facing each another, with one person at the head. These people will catch the faller. Faller stands with her back to the catchers, feet planted. She will fall directly backwards, with her body in one piece, no bends, not collapsing. The catchers extend their arms, palms up, ready to catch. Watch that catchers' heads are back, out of the way of the faller. All check to make sure they're ready before giving the faller the signal to let go. Faller is given 2 or 3 seconds of free fall before being caught and lowered gently to the mat or brought back to standing after going part way down. It's fun to have faller and/or catchers release a sound with the movement.

This can also be done with just 3 catchers and one faller, if players are comfortable with that. Also, a 2-person version is to have a player tilt back, keeping her feet on the floor, giving her weight to her partner with the catcher lowering the faller as much or as little as feels safe to them. There are moments in scenes when falling and catching can create an intimate and dramatic image.

> *Play is the highest form of research.*
>
> —*Albert Einstein*

GROUP YES
Beginner / Intermediate

(A Keith Johnstone exercise.)

This is a game for ensembles that explores the relationship between individual preference and "group mind." Good to do this after all are warmed up and moving in ensemble, on their feet, spread throughout the studio. One person at a time, on impulse, calls out a suggestion for an action such as: "Everyone collapse onto the floor" or "Everyone sing an operatic aria."

All those who like the suggestion and want to do it, go ahead and do it. These actors call out loudly "Yes," as they enact their version of the action. Those who don't want to do it just wait for the next suggestion, preferably soon offering one of their own. The group stays with the action they're doing until a new one is offered. It's interesting to see what actions are most accepted and for each player to sense the will of the group.

AUTHENTIC MOVEMENT. We usually do an Authentic Movement exercise by class number two and often repeat this technique for self-connection at all levels of practice. As defined on an Authentic Movement website, Authentic Movement is a simple form of self-directed movement. It's usually done with eyes closed and attention directed inward, in the presence of at least one witness. Movers explore spontaneous gestures, movements and stillness, following inner impulses in the present moment. The witness watches and tracks inner responses to the mover with the intention of not judging, but focusing on self-awareness. It is a meditative, spiritual practice that integrates body and mind for increased access to consciousness. The particular relationship between mover and witness, in moving and being seen by another, creates a powerful framework within which this work takes place. A.M. can be done as part of psychotherapy process, for enhanced sense of self and well-being and as artistic support, to connect with the creative process, unblocking and opening to new ideas and impulses. Often the experience of Authentic Movement feels like meaningful play and is full of fun. At other times movers and witnesses experience intense feelings and helpful insights into the wisdom of their own bodies." In pairs, one mover, one witness. The class spreads out and students focus on their partner. After Apple has moved for 4-8 minutes, stop and let her report her experience to her partner. Then her partner can say what she saw and her response. Take no more than 2 minutes for talking. Then switch roles. For students with little or no creative movement training, this is a pleasurable way to increase awareness of both body and mind and to practice focusing on the experience of movement rather than the appearance of it. They often find this to be a surprisingly revealing and inspiring activity.

KEEPING GOING

Two roles: the walker and the impulse-giver/director, A and B. The walker (A) walks around the studio, establishing a brisk, regular pace, with the intention of going somewhere. The director (B) follows and touches the walker on various places on her body, to direct her to change tempo or direction and put the mover's body in new shapes. B may lift the walker's arm and drop it gently or take the arm and pull the mover around, creating spin. She may give the receiver a push from behind on her mid back or neck or shoulder or knee. The touches should vary in intensity and placement. The walker responds without resistance but keeps her forward momentum going as well, so that when not being touched she's moving on her own direction. We're practicing combining self-intention with openness and response to a partner's offers. After 4-5 minutes, switch A and B. Establish new roles. Then we'll add sound, on the contact, on the touch. Either or both players may release a sound response along with the movement.

I might narrate the next phase like this: "Then you'll switch A and B on your impulse. I'm not going to tell you. You'll just walk and make it clear that, OK, now I'm the walker. The change may be smooth or it may be awkward. Either way is fine. Just switch roles whenever you want to. Keep the sound if you can. And change partners. Feel free to break up a pair. Just cut in like at a dance, tapping someone on the shoulder, and that's your partner. Use the whole space. As you're moving, try to have a sense of all the moving bodies. Let your radar and sonar be on. As you're playing with your partner, that's your main point of concentration, your partner, but there is some concentration left for awareness of what's going on in the whole room. In an ensemble, we want awareness of the whole. Change partners whenever you like. It doesn't matter if you worked with the person before. You can pick them up again."

(When ready to conclude:) "We'll take ten seconds for the whole ensemble to come to stillness together. Begin to sense all your partners. You're going to gradually come to complete stillness in unison. Notice the image the group creates in the final composition."

THE OBSERVER / SPATIAL AWARENESS

This can be done (and repeated) any time the ensemble is moving freely around the space. "As you're moving about the studio, notice the space between you and others, notice that it feels different when you pass someone closely, how the air between you is charged. Imagine that you're making lines in the space like painted paths on the floor and notice that you're creating patterns as an ensemble, a kind of choreography. Now, freeze in place, close your eyes, and relax for a few seconds. Then imagine that you can fly up to the roof and look down through it to see this whole space. You have a bird's-eye view of everyone and everything. You can see where you are in the room, how close you are to the walls, to the other bodies. Can you see who's next to you? Who is behind you? OK, now open your eyes and look around. How accurate were you? Now, go back to moving. Is your spatial awareness sharper?" Developing this awareness is necessary for improvisers to spontaneously create provocative and artful visual images.

INSTANT DREAMS

After doing a physically demanding exercise, students need to pause and rest. Have all drop to the floor and take a "one-minute nap." Usually I'll start making snoring sounds, and within a few seconds most of the people are contributing to the delightful orchestra of sleep sounds. After a couple of minutes (again, the length of any activity depends on the energy of the moment, so if all are happily engaged on the floor in a snoring symphony, don't cut it off), when the sounding energy begins to wane, say, "One at a time, please jump up and tell us your dream. Tell a dream you've had or make one up." Students drop back down to the floor when finished with dream. This usually takes about 40–90 seconds per person. I do this in beginner and advanced classes and am often delighted by the imaginative little stories told.

MIRROR AND VARIATIONS

This class of exercises is used in every improv training I've heard of. Mirror is a simple game that is wonderful for concentration and connection. I use it in all beginner classes, but it's useful at all levels when connection and focus are needed.

When I was teaching drama to children in public and private schools through LEAP: Imagination in Learning, I was once asked to teach a Special Education class of 14 students with severe behavior problems. I wasn't trained in this kind of teaching but I gave it a try and found it incredibly difficult. (Special Ed teachers are heroic! Thankfully, two of them were in the room with me.) Just to get the kids, ages 9-11, to form a circle took me 10 minutes of wrangling. Once they were in a circle, it was nearly impossible to get them to follow instructions. The circle would dissolve. I tried a variety of exercises, most of which they refused to do or would try out for 1-2 minutes then leave the group and run about the room, climbing on the desks, throwing books, pencils, etc. Chaos. The one structure that worked every time was Mirror. I taught them the exercise and told them that the idea was to move so simultaneously that I could not tell who was leading and who was following. They took up this challenge and would play mirror in pairs for as long as 20 minutes. They were also willing to play a variation of mirror: the children's game, Who Started the Motion? (See below.) Mirror moves players into a sort of low trance state, which was calming to the students. (I didn't last long teaching this class. Sadly, I quit after 3 weeks.)

BASIC MIRROR EXERCISE
Pairs

The group, in pairs, spreads out in the space. They decide who is going to be the mover (A) and who is will be the mirror reflection (B). The two stand facing each other, about 4 feet apart, and the mirror tries to create a true reflection of the person facing her. Players make eye contact and maintain that most of the time they are playing.

The instructions to Apple are: move slowly and continuously and with variety, in any way you like. For Banana: reflect the movements of your partner as closely as you can. The mover slowly begins to move, and the mirror reflects her movements, trying to move simultaneously with her partner. Remind players that when looking directly ahead (into partner's eyes) you can see enough of your partner's body with your peripheral vision to be with her. If necessary, you can very briefly glance down or to the side. If A is losing B, if they are not in sync, the movements need to be simpler and slower. Both hold the intention to stay together. It's best to start out with abstract movement, as it's less predictable than naturalistic moves, such as brushing your teeth or waving to someone. After the exercise is underway the teacher can suggest endowing the action with emotion.

After a while, ask the actors to switch; the mover becomes the mirror, and vice versa. This can be done without a break in the flow of actions.

Once the exercise moves into the changeover without a break in the flow, have them switch roles without the leader telling them. They switch back and forth on impulse. Both partners can initiate and/or reflect at all times. There is no longer any distinction; both are A and both are B.

CHANGING MIRRORS

Start the actors working in Free Mirror then tell them that at your signal they are to break eye contact with their partners, and, from wherever they are, look for new partners. These changes of partners can be repeated a number of times, until the teacher ends the exercise. This works well as a segue into Eye-Contact/No-Eye-Contact Journey (below).

ALL FOLLOW ONE, OR WHO STARTED THE MOTION?
In a Circle

This is another reflecting game, in which one person in the circle is the initiator of a repeated movement pattern and the group mirrors him. Then a new initiator emerges and the group immediately recognizes the change and unifies, all doing the same moves in unison.

All mirror exercises require intense concentration and observation of others, so should be followed by a short periods of non-relating and releasing, with actors moving about the studio indulging their individual needs.

EYE CONTACT / NO EYE CONTACT JOURNEY. Intermediate/Advanced. This is done in ensemble, after warm-up. Find a partner and then spread around the space. Start by making eye contact with your partner. You'll maintain this eye contact for a while, and you're going to open the eyes in the back of your head and turn on your radar and sonar so that you can move through space while still maintaining eye contact with your partner 98 percent of the time. Play with the distance between the two of you and the feeling between you. This eye contact is like a bridge or a line of energy between you and your partner. It's your connecting cord, so to speak. Let yourself be varying distances from your partner, sometimes very close, sometimes across the whole room. Vary the dynamic, the intensity, and the tempo of your movement. You're staying with one partner with eye contact and seeing the rest of the players with your peripheral vision. Sometimes eye contact can seem very personal. See if you can notice how that happens for you, what feelings or associations come up about it, what images. Just notice them. They're fruitful. There's drama in them. Maybe you're comfortable with the eye contact at some times, not at others. If needed, of course, you can break the contact for a few seconds here and there. After a while, you'll keep playing with your partner, with this stimulus response, but you'll look anywhere except your partner's face. Eye contact is not available to you now. You can see your partner with your peripheral vision and kinesthetically, you can sense his presence in the room and where he is in relation to you, always. So there's that sending and receiving loop between you and your partner. No matter where you are in the space you are radiating energy to your partner. If there's an impulse to touch, go ahead, that's another connection—body contact. Travel together through the space, try different levels, just don't look in your partner's eyes. Remember that this is a conversation between the two of you. You are always affected by your partner. Go as far as you can with the impulses that are coming up. Make strong offers. You're both leading and following. (After 4-5 minutes:) Now you may look in your partner's face if you need to. You have all these modes of connection now: looking briefly in your partner's eyes, communicating through the body, through energy and touch. If you find you need to make sounds, do that, release the sound. (After another 3-4 minutes, a 10 second warning should be given for coming to stillness.) Then, each pair will perform with the group witnessing (possibly with new partners). They will start a new eye contact/no eye contact journey and begin to introduce more sound and some language. Side coach: Is there anything that you need to say with your voice to your partner, either with sound or with words? Is there some image that is coming up, that is driving a verbal utterance or a vocal utterance? Speak when you need to. Remember, use the whole space. (This practice will create short physical theatre pieces.)

VOCAL MIRROR
Beginner / Intermediate, pairs

A vocal/verbal version of mirror, with the same set up in which the pairs facing each other focus on the partner's mouth and speak in unison. The same progression applies, starting with an assigned leader and progressing to passing the roles back and forth. Initiators must speak slowly and commit to staying in sync with their partners. It's good to change leaders in the middle of sentences.

TWO AS ONE SPEECHES OR STORIES
Beginner / Intermediate, pairs

This performance structure comes out of Vocal Mirror. Two players stand center stage, about two feet apart, slightly facing each other, in a kind of open V shape, so that they can easily swivel their heads to see one another and to look out at the audience. They are to assume that they are one person (with two heads) and speak in the singular "I." The leader (or a third student) will introduce the players to the audience by saying, "Professor Hutzenklutzen (any made-up name) has come to speak with us today. Welcome, Professor." Or something like that. Then the actors will begin their speech or story, using vocal mirror to speak in unison. They will surprise themselves and the witnesses if they pass the leadership back and forth often. This is a light, fun exercise that intensely practices concentration and co-operation. The results are often very funny.

> *Logic will get you from A to B.*
> *Imagination will take you everywhere.*
>
> *—Albert Einstein*

YES, AND

Beginners, 3–5 players

With the recent popularity of comedy improv, the YES, AND principle has become pretty well known. Here's a very simple, basic exercise to practice YES, AND verbal responses to partners' offers.

Three, four, or five students get up in front of the class. They are to solve a problem collaboratively. The teacher gives them an identity as a group of people who would work together, such as the board of supervisors of a city. They're also given a problem, such as:

"A UFO has landed in the plaza" or "There's a garbage strike and the streets are filled with trash." The players are told to offer their ideas to solve the problem by tossing them out, in any order, in response to what was just said. They must begin each of their verbal offers with the words "Yes, and..." For example, for the strike, the first player might say:

A: I think we should have a garbage sculpture contest.

B: Yes, great idea, and we'll give first prize to the person who uses the most garbage.

C: Yes, and a special prize for making a sculpture that doesn't smell bad.

D: Yes, and one of the prizes will consist of open access to the dump, where the artists can have any material they want.

And so on.

I rarely offer students the given circumstances of a piece (who and what, in this case) but do so just to keep their concentration focused on the YES, AND task. This is a fundamental exercise that reveals to new students something about their habitual responses to offers. It's so common to say no, to argue with your partners (in life as well as on stage) because it's a way to assert oneself and to create conflict, which, in fact, we value in drama and which some people enjoy in life. So it must be explained to new improvisers that while we need to cooperate in the creation of a piece of theatre, we can agree to create conflict and trouble within the story of the piece.

GIBBERISH TRANSLATOR
Beginner / Intermediate, pairs.

The whole class practices speaking gibberish (nonsense language) while milling about as though at a party. They should be coached to use a variety of sounds. This will be easy for some, very difficult for others. Actors should have a sense of what they mean to say. This is a fundamental acting exercise, as meaning must be conveyed through vocal and emotional life. I often observe new students' greater intensity of feeling when speaking gibberish than when speaking English.

Then the pairs are onstage, one playing a foreign speaker who has come to address the audience, the other the translator. One character speaks no English, only gibberish. The translator, of course, speaks both languages and will translate for the audience. If the two speak to each other they, of course, speak in gibberish. Remind them that this is a collaboration: although the translator can say anything she wants, she should take her cues from the foreign speaker's behavior and her partner will respond to her translation. The gibberish speaker should be very physically active, thereby giving her partner much to respond to. The translator is not to worry about understanding exactly what his partner has in mind. He just goes with his own interpretation. Incongruities between what is heard by the audience and what the translator says will likely create humor. For example: if the foreign speaker gives a long, impassioned speech and his partner translates it as; "He says maybe, maybe not."

If students feel awkward and limited speaking gibberish, remind them that that they can practice nonsense language at home or while driving.

Reflect, Extend, Respond. Since all you can do with another improviser is reflect or extend or respond, this practices lively physical theatre relationships. It's also a way to begin a duo or trio piece. It's a great group warm up before a performance. This should be done after having practiced Mirror, Leader/Follower, Circle Stimulus/Response, Eye Contact to No Eye Contact and Keeping Going. It's fruitful to repeat this structure often.

In pairs or threes: one is A, the initiator; B is responder. If there are 3 players, there will be two bananas. Apple begins to move, enacting his psychophysical and vocal impulses, constantly monitoring himself to avoid self-blocking. Best for A not to look much at his partner, neither should he try to avoid looking. He's just focusing on what needs to be expressed. Banana takes all her cues from Apple by reflecting, extending, and responding to A's actions. After 3-5 minutes, switch roles. Then, after another 3-5 minutes, the leader says, "Now you are both A and both B, reflecting, extending, responding."

THE SWAMP
Intermediate / Advanced

Once improvisers are moving freely in group awareness around the studio doing Reflect, Extend, Respond, the leader can suggest changing partners on impulse and then, after a while: "Thinking of everyone on the floor as your partner, activate your spatial awareness to let in the whole ensemble. Enjoy the sense of being part of the whole." Remind players to explore timing, speed, dynamic (tension, release, soft, hard, sharp, round...) and stillness. Add in the option of sound. Add in the possibility of players coming and going, leaving the floor and returning, creating solos and clusters. Move in natural rhythms, fall in and out of partnerships. Make space for brief verbal and or vocal solos to emerge as the ensemble supports the soloist. The group energy will create a bubbling, organic ensemble composition that I like to call The Swamp. When it seems time to close the event, ask improvisers to find their way to stillness, creating a tableau, as a unit.

> *It is the imagination that should be awakened and trained.*
>
> —*Carl Orff*

COMEDIA DELL'ARTE PHYSICAL THEATRE RIFFS
Pairs

You've likely seen these bits if you've ever watched Laurel and Hardy or Charlie Chaplin or our contemporary clown, Bill Irwin (from whom I learned them).

Students are in pairs with A directly in front of B. A walks forward in a regular, brisk tempo with B following closely behind, in lock step with A. B stays in step with A, stops when A stops, changes gait or tempo with A and keeps the space between them constant. Then A swivels around and B is now the leader. This can be done with A looking behind and "not seeing" B.

Variations: Players walk, run in slo-mo, march in lockstep, or travel back-to-back or face-to-face (one moves backward). Face-to-face moving together is very useful in scenes.

We want to notice opportunities to join partners in unison movement. It's so satisfying to see people move in sync and so much fun to do. I suggest students learn to dance together, waltz or any other ballroom dance, so they can break into dance if the scene invites it.

CUTTING LOOSE
Intermediate / Advanced

This exercise will create a series of solos within ensemble.

All move about the studio at your own pace with your radar and sonar turned on. As you walk, notice your mood and imagine that you are going somewhere so that your walk has intention. You'll be minimally influenced by the movement around you. At some point, one improviser will break out of her regular walk and cut loose, finding a highly charged impulse that wants to be released in the form of movement, sound and (possibly, but not necessarily) words. Allow this to be "crazy" behavior, triggered by a sensation in the body or the image or thought of something in your life that frustrates or stimulates you. You'll have a kind of freak out or meltdown enacted with unrestrained energy. The ensemble's attention will be drawn to the "crazy" person until she's finished with her action, so players will slow down enough to observe her fully. Then another player will catch the "crazy bug" and indulge in his own outburst, letting himself be triggered by the previous person's behavior. When all have had a turn to solo, each improviser will find a partner with whom to have a "crazy" behavior interaction. At the end of the exercise all will lie on the floor (or mats) to have a one-minute "digesting experience" and rest. This behavior may shine a light on parts of the self that usually don't get much exposure and will likely be useful to draw on in performance.

> *Full-blown artistic creativity takes place when a trained and skilled grownup is able to tap the source of clear, unbroken, play consciousness of the small child within.*

—*Stephen Nachmanovitch, in* Free Play, Improvisation in Life and Art

I FEEL
Beginners, pairs

This exercise is used as needed for students who, when asked what they're feeling or wanting, say that they don't know. Or the teacher may observe that a student has low affect and appears to be emotionally blocked. The student who finds it challenging to reveal feeling may be paired with a more experienced or uninhibited person and both must receive lots of support and empathy from the teacher and class.

Two players stand face to face about four feet apart. They both close their eyes for a few seconds and check into themselves, trying to identify their predominant feeling(s) of the moment. Then #1 reports to #2 how he feels, i.e.: "I feel nervous" or "I feel excited," etc. #2 lets his partner's offer land and then responds with what he feels. Students should try to reveal their feelings through gesture, and/or movement and breath, as well as words.

CONNECTIONS
Beginning / Intermediate, 6 to 20 actors

My variation of the exercise Crossings, from *An Acrobat of The Heart*, this is a basic self-awareness and stimulus-response exercise.

Tell students that there are two tasks for Connections:

1. Connect with your partner.

2. Do only what you want to do.

Divide the group in half and have actors line up laterally, each person facing a partner across the room. Ask players to imagine a path, about four feet wide, crossing the space, connecting each person to their partner.

Each turn away from your partner for a few seconds and check in with yourself. Then turn around and face your partner. When both of you have turned toward each other, make eye contact. Try to maintain eye contact throughout the exercise, when it feels right. If it feels forced, release your eyes and notice where they focus next. You can reestablish eye contact any time.

You will move toward or away from your partner staying within your path. Either person can move toward or away from the other at any time, on impulse; just be sure that after each step you notice what you're feeling. If your partner moves, check in with yourself. What is your reaction? Which way do you want to move now? If you don't know which way to move, stop and check in to feel your impulse. Trust your instincts. If you feel like moving away, try turning away from your partner or turn sideways. If your partner turns her back on you, you may move around in front of her. If you feel shy or playful, let it show.

Remember that the primary tasks are to try to connect with your partner while doing only what feels authentic to you. You're getting to know your partner and learning more about yourself. Even when you break eye contact, try to stay as connected as you were when your eyes were locked with your partner's. Try changing levels. Looking up or down at your partner changes your relationship radically. Try possibly sitting, crawling and lying down, as well as standing. You will need to "listen" with your whole body. Try different tempos of movement.

If you and your partner get close enough to touch, search for a way to touch each other that feels safe and comfortable. If, while searching for a touch, you feel you want to step back, do. You may find that your partner wants to hug but you don't feel like it. Or vice versa. You can gently move out of reach. And if you and your partner never get close enough to touch, that's fine, just keep moving towards and away. If you find a satisfactory touch, sense for how long this wants to last. The teacher will let you know when to end and you can then find a goodbye gesture for your partner and make your way back to your starting place. You may find that you feel guilty for not hugging your partner or have hurt feelings that he didn't want to hug you. See if you can not take any of this personally. After the teacher calls release you can talk briefly with your partner. Next, move the lines so that each person has a new partner and do the exercise again. Notice how unique each relationship is.

At a certain point you may feel that you are simply responding honestly to your partner and the impulses may come more quickly. The idea is that over time you will feel, immediately, what's real for you in your body and psyche, and the process of self-awareness will be internalized and instinctive.

DIRECTORS AND NOUNS

The next two exercises practice expanding expressive range and spontaneity.

Pairs or Trios

A is the director; B is the actor. The director will choose 5 nouns, either abstract nouns like: ambition, suspicion, curiosity, confusion, or concrete nouns: river, baby, money, storm. The actor will stand in centered neutral, ready to receive. Director says one of the nouns and actor responds to the word immediately, on impulse, with no time to think. Let the action be primarily physical. Use words if you really need to. When you feel your action is complete, come back to neutral and the director will say the next word. This can be done in trio with two actors and one director.

Follow with this exercise:

DIRECTORS AND CHANGE
Pairs or Trios

A is the director; B is the actor. The actor takes a moment to center, find out what's happening for him, and then starts any kind of behavior that's very physical and vocal, encompasses the whole being and has a particular emotional tone. The action is going to be one beat/one impulse and, at a certain point, your director is going to say, "Change," and you'll switch to a contrasting behavior. Don't think opposites because it's hard to tell what opposite means, just think contrasting action. The director will say "Change" four times, which will create five behaviors. Everybody take one area of the room. The directors are practicing sensing for, "When's the right time to say change?" and, "Is that action fully expressed?" It's just one impulse, one action, so if it's fully expressed we're not going to give it a chance to transform to a new beat. When the director feels that one action is complete, he'll say, "Change." When the actor has created five actions, switch roles. This also can be done in trios with two actors and one director. After both these actor/director exercises, have the players talk to each other for a minute, reporting what they experienced and what they observed.

OVER-ACCEPTING
Pairs

This is an exercise that practices developing verbal offers. Partners face each other; decide A and B.

A makes a statement, an observation or opinion, such as, "It's so hot in here today!"

B responds with huge emotion and physical gesture and riffs on the suggested reality.

"It's sooo hot that I think my face is beginning to melt. As a matter of fact, this is what I imagine hell feels like…" and continues free associating, until he's ready to switch roles with A.

This is a supported solo—an exercise, not a scene—so B just receives and responds emotionally, not verbally. We are practicing receiving and developing offers.

When it's A's turn to over-accept, B's new statement/observation, for his partner, will come out of his rant: "Come to think of it, you look like the devil."

A picks it up and runs with it:

"You found me out, even in my best disguise! Diablo, that's me. Well, baby, live with it, I can't hide it any longer…"

Players should go as far as they can with these riffs. Usually students stop well before they've really let loose. They can almost always go farther if pushed a bit.

DEVELOP THAT

Pairs: Director and Mover

Here's an exercise in extending and developing physical riffs.

Mover moves according to her impulses, taking an attitude of exploration. Director watches, letting the mover get going for at least 30 seconds before intervening. When the director sees some movement or gesture that interests him, he says, "Develop that." The mover then repeats, explores, clarifies and deepens her gestures and whole body moves until it transforms into a new image/feeling. The director is watching for this change and when he sees it, says, "Develop that" again. At the end of the mover's turn, the two players take no more than a minute or so to give feedback. Each tells the director how it was for her, what she learned. Director says what he saw. Then switch roles. This can also be done with two interacting movers and one director, a good way to practice movement awareness in scenes. Also, when players are performing, the director or teacher may coach them to develop any movement that she feels has possibilities to enrich the piece.

LET YOUR PARTNER CHANGE YOU

Pairs (Performance Structure)

This structure practices the fundamental, essential phenomenon of stimulus/response: the basic action of every improvised piece. This is the first scene structure taught in FSI training and can be usefully practiced again and again. This is transcribed from class:

Start in opposite corners, one upstage right, one downstage left (or vice versa). When you find your place, take a few seconds to check into what's going on for you emotionally. A soon as you have that, move out into the playing space while you physicalize and intensify that feeling. Though you may find more than one emotion available to you, pick the strongest one and be sure it's clear and committed. The other feelings will likely be revealed as well and give subtext to your behavior. As soon as you're "onstage," look at your partner across the space and let your partner in. What do you read about her? What is your response? Your material is what is actually going on. If you find a way to express that clearly and physically, you are going to know what to do because your offers are coming from your real reaction to your partner. At first, these pieces will be short: 3-5 minutes. You'll end up at the other end of the stage, where your partner started, and she'll end up where you started, so you'll make a journey across the space. And by the time you're finished, you will have gone through numerous changes, so that by the end you will be in a different condition than you were when you started. We'll do the first round with no language. You'll create a physical narrative. Later we'll repeat the structure and include words.

If the players lose their connection to their psychophysical selves when they start to speak, the leader should stop them and ask them to restart with no language or have them include the Physical/Emotional Life First technique in their piece.

IN-CLASS DISCUSSION RE LET YOUR PARTNER CHANGE YOU

Patty: What I got from it was to allow my partner's reactions to affect my response. But I felt kind of shy at the beginning and sort of self-protective, so I don't think I really let her in.

Joya: Patty, when you started, I didn't quite read what your emotion was. It was a little foggy to me and usually that's because there's one thing you are feeling and another thing you're trying to project. Maybe there's some kind of judgment about what you are actually feeling. Often there's a fear that people could judge our shadow side as negative. We don't have that in theatre. Feelings are feelings; we don't believe that on stage that rage is any worse than peace or that euphoria is better than frustration. Those are just colors of the palette. So, if you find yourself feeling shy or furious, let us see that clearly. Don't pull your punches. Reveal it; clarify it. Often with the shadow side, people try to mitigate it or cover it up and then you get this kind of murkiness because, in improvisation, you can't actually hide what you are feeling. Of course, you will often have more than one feeling but you can only physicalize one at a time. The underlying feelings will be felt and will make your presence more interesting. If you intensify your feelings, your partner, and the audience, are more likely to get it. You want to give your partner something clear to work with. Your whole reality is there and she has her reality, and the relationship comes from that. If you're as truthful as you can be, transformation will come easily, the reality will change, and there will be a new feeling and a new beat.

Patty: I've seen that in other scenes. I just didn't feel real connected to my partner.

Joya: Well, that happens, especially when you're hiding. When in doubt about connection, remember eye contact. And again, let your longing for connection, or your fear of it, or your frustration about it, show. Let that be part of the action of the scene.

Let's do one more round with a different partner. And this time, I want you to focus a lot on your relationship, really noticing what she's feeling and every time your response changes, I want to see that. I want you to be as physically expressive as possible. Then we are going to do a third round adding language. Always, when you are practicing, the bottom line is, "What's true for me?" You want to keep getting in touch with your intuition.

SILENT TENSION
Intermediate / Advanced, pairs or trios.

A variation of a Viola Spolin exercise: improvised scenes creating narrative without words. I describe it as: "Two or three people with so much emotional charge between them that they are unable to speak." Players come in with a clear and intense emotional state. This may be practiced as a scene with one given circumstance, such as; "This is your ex-lover," or "You are siblings," or "You're wildly attracted to him," or an objective may be suggested, such as "You want her off your back." For more advanced players it should be done without predetermined content or circumstances.

Try the whole scene with no language and ask players to sense for a beginning, middle and end. Breath sounds and crying, moaning, laughing, are encouraged from the top of the scene and throughout. Silent Tension is also a great way to begin a piece, committed to physical life, in which language is used later in the scene, when the improvisers feel a great need to speak.

*People wish to be settled: only as far as they are unsettled
is there any hope for them.*

—*Ralph Waldo Emerson*

WEST SIDE STORY
Beginner / Intermediate, 8–16 players

This exercise, as the name suggests, is based on the musical play West Side Story.

Divide the group in half and have them line up laterally, each person facing their partner across the room. The folks on the same side of the room are a team (or a gang, as in the Jets and the Sharks). Have about 2 feet of space on both sides of each team member. The person at the end of the line of team A will travel across the room to confront the team member opposite him. He will offer a gesture and sound, and possibly a few words, as a challenge. Example: "Hey big boy. Ya think yer tough?" His locomotion will be stylized: sauntering, skipping, sneaking, moving aggressively. The receiver will respond in a similar style.

Then the initiator will return to his team (who has been watching attentively) and the whole gang will repeat the action, hopefully in unison, each delivered to their opponents. Team B members may each respond organically, in their own way. Then the first actor in gang B travels across to deliver his greeting. Each player has a turn and takes his team with him. We want this to look like choreographed ensemble movement. Players must use their peripheral vision and sonar to stay in step with their colleagues.

BLIND LEADING BLIND
6–16 players

Make a circle in which all hold hands. Then break open the circle into a line. Have all close their eyes and take a moment to center and relax. Then, as a unit, the group will move through the studio, slowly, staying in physical contact. Players may let go of hands and be touching side-to-side or back-to-back, so that the line can morph into a clump that moves together. Each must always be touching at least 2 other people. As the "blind" group explores the space, the leader will monitor for safety. Wonderful for kinesthetic awareness and building group trust.

> **Stupid Dance:** All make a circle. Play some pop music with a regular beat or some jazz or vary the music, including some with slow tempo. One person at a time goes into the center and dances in as silly a way as possible. The objective is to look stupid, awkward—to "make a fool of yourself," the thing that almost all of us are afraid to do. People in the circle copy the center person's movement as closely as possible. The dancers should be coached: "No graceful moves, nothing pretty or hip, please." This exercise is really fun and provokes a lot of very free movement and a lot of laughter.

EMOTION DANCE

Emotion Dance is a variation of the above that keeps the circle structure. The teacher/director calls out to the lead player an emotion or mode of movement, such as hysterical, confused, euphoric, repressed, languid, as he's dancing in the center of the circle.

BAD ACTING

In a similar vein to Stupid Dance: in the center of circle, do a brief performance (solo, duo or trio) that's as broad and corny and "over the top" as you can make it. Actors take turns being in the center with each piece being influenced by the piece that went before. This exercise addresses the common tendency to hold back for fear of "over-acting." There's a truism in acting training that I subscribe to: "You can always pull it back, when you have something big to work with." I think the fear of over-acting is actually the legitimate desire to avoid untruthful acting. We want improvisers to feel comfortable in many styles of acting.

EMPTY VESSEL

My adaptation of this exercise from Ruth Zaporah's Action Theater technique focuses on joining and intensifying your partner's reality. It can be done with 2 to 4 players (3 is my favorite).

One actor is the Empty Vessel, who will receive offers, one at a time, from each partner in turn. A approaches the vessel (the receiver) with an offer in the form of movement, sound and/or language and clear emotional life.

Example: A is laughing hysterically about something that happened to her. B (the Vessel), who has been standing in centered neutral, responds to the offer by joining in and intensifies the laughter, her whole body engaged. The actors are not mirroring each other but are joining in the same mode of behavior. Dialogue may emerge, but is not necessary.

The Vessel follows A's lead. The two expand the impulse until player C, who has been observing and letting the action play through him, comes in, replacing B with his new offer. He will enter when he feels the action is complete enough to offer a new beat. His offer will be triggered by the behavior he just observed. Each pairing creates only one beat, so each action will likely take 30-60 seconds.

After all improvisers have had a turn being the Empty Vessel, go on to the next phase of the exercise. This time, when A's offer has been developed, she and B let their impulses segue them on to the next beat (preferably a contrasting behavior) and new actions emerge. So, first the players are enacting the same behaviors, then different. It becomes obvious to the actors that if they explore one impulse as long as needed, the next beat will arise organically. When that happens, players' responses will create a short mini scene. The scene continues when the next player enters with a new offer. When all have had a turn being the Empty Vessel, the exercise ends.

If you are not affected by what you see,
what you touch, what you feel, what you notice,
what is the difference between you and a stone?

—*Guru Nitya Chaitanya Yati*

ONE MOVES—ONE TALKS
Beginner / Intermediate, pairs

This playful exercise separates the elements of verbal life and physical life and practices transitioning from one to the other. Both moving and speaking are, of course, endowed and motivated by emotion and inner imagery. This can be practiced in pairs by the whole class at once, and then done with pairs being witnessed by the group.

In this structure there are two roles that must be filled at all times: the mover and the talker. The talker must stand in one spot, feet glued to the floor, but able to move her upper body. The mover may do anything with her body. If the talker stops speaking and begins to move about, she is in the role of mover, so the mover now becomes the talker. The players listen and respond to one another, letting the verbal life affect the movement and the movement affect the verbal life. Either player can initiate the change of roles at any time. Verbal life may be a continuous monologue, with one improviser picking up where the other left off or it may be a dialogue between the players. Content will emerge organically. Concentrating on a simple form, as this exercise does, will sometimes result in players having little mental energy left to worry about the text, which is a good thing.

Variations on this exercise: Both Move/One Talks, Both Talk and Move at the same time, (This requires big listening and orchestrating the rhythm and volume of the language.) Also try one moving as the other provides sound accompaniment while moving or still. Of course, in performance, improvisers will use and mix all these elements intuitively.

MOVE ON EVERY NEW BEAT
Intermediate / Advanced, 2–3 players

A technique used to create interesting and meaningful spatial composition in performance.

Actors begin a scene and are asked to notice every time the beat changes. They are to change their spatial relationship on every new beat. It's a good time to talk about how spatial relationships reveal connection and attitude of the characters, how different it is to be with someone across the room from you, as contrasted to speaking two inches apart, or with your back to the other person or with one sitting and one standing. Remind folks that theatre is a visual medium. They will be composing stage pictures and imagery that evoke meaning.

SPACE / SHAPE
Pairs

We often do the Space/Shape exercise with a chair before doing Repetition (below). It's another version of Move on Every New Beat.

Each pair has one chair. They create a dialogue with no language, responding to each other's offers physically, being particularly aware of their spatial relationship. The chair is used to define the space and to provide possibilities for varied body shapes, and imagery. Encourage actors to play with the chair in every way that occurs to them. This is also a good introduction to prop exploration.

REPETITION
Beginner / Intermediate, pairs

Though Sanford Meisner's fundamental acting exercise is also called Repetition, this exercise, while related, is something else. This is a good structure to use in beginner classes for an intro to creating scenes/pieces. It relieves players of the need to create text and demonstrates that acting is not really about the words. It's about the meaning under the words, which may or may not be spoken.

The teacher gives both players the same one phrase that serves as their entire script. This pushes them to communicate primarily through physical/emotional life and use of space. The idea is that the essential thing you're doing in a scene is re-acting/responding. Emphasize connection with, and observation of, each other. Improvisers will discover that the story of the scene develops as the relationship progresses and that they can create a relationship without a lot of words. Give the players a simple phrase such as, "I see you're wearing that shirt again tonight." and ask them to both use only those words when they need to speak. After the whole sentence is spoken at least twice by each, they may break it down and say only some of the words: "I see!" "...again tonight?" etc. How the actor/character feels about what he's received will be revealed through his delivery. This is subtext. As the scene progresses, the teacher may side-coach: "Feel free to add a new phrase." If one actor speaks new words they then have two phrases. The actors may feel frustrated with the limited text. They can be coached to use the energy of the frustration in their communication with their partner. Remind them that they can speak volumes with their bodies and radiated feelings.

PHYSICAL LIFE & EMOTIONAL LIFE FIRST IN SCENES

By now it's obvious that the primacy of physical and emotional life in theatre is a core principle in FSI. In this improvisation, all verbal exchanges are preceded by physical movement or gesture, with the understanding that most movement will be motivated by feeling. Why I say "most movement" instead of "all," is that sometimes gesture or shape is a part of stage picture/composition, created for visual aesthetic purposes, still meant to reveal meaning.

This is also a good exercise to use with written text, as it slows down the dialogue process to clarify each beat and endows verbal life with physical subtext. Actors and the audience may enjoy very fast-paced, clever verbal repartee, especially when the piece is comedic, but speed may make it difficult to allow for a deep level of feeling in a more dramatic piece. Of course, there are exceptions to that, such as an angry or excited verbal exchange, which are naturally fast and in which people often speak over one another. In this case, physical life will likely be fast moving.

This technique should be practiced often, as it's the habit of most people to rely heavily on language for meaning. After all, we're in conversations (having them, hearing them) every day of our lives. We're deeply familiar with dialogue. Once improvisers have the habit of embodied acting, they will not need to always create physical actions before they speak. (That could be quite a burden, couldn't it?) When creating a piece in performance, there will be times when you will stand or sit, stock still, with arms at your side, just speaking. Even then (especially then), you want your body to radiate a particular kind of energy.

We don't want to lean too heavily on language as the foremost ingredient of ensemble improv theatre because our text is not usually as well written as a good play that has been rewritten and edited. Improvised text is a first draft. That said, though it's quite challenging, I've seen and heard and created many improvised stories and scenes in which the language is rich and articulate and sometimes poetic. We certainly strive for that skill.

Albert Mehrabian, a pioneer in the field of nonverbal communication, says his research reveals that about 7 percent of our feelings are carried by words. The tone of our voice reveals about 38 percent of communication, and 55 percent is conveyed by body language.

TECHNIQUES OF "FIGHTING," "KILLING," "DYING" OR BEING "DRUNK" OR "STONED" ON STAGE

Improvisers practice slow-motion fighting and fighting with no body contact. A rule of thumb for hitting one's partner is that the receiver of the abuse controls the action by reacting to his partner's touch in ways that demonstrate impact. For example: person being strangled writhes back and forth with his hand on his throat creating the illusion of being pushed about, while the "aggressor" gently holds his hands below partner's throat. If you are "hitting" another player, you do not actually touch them. The person being punched or kicked responds, as if hit, by recoiling from the blow. Obviously, no one should actually get hurt when acting aggression on stage. Safety is essential.

We may kill each other on stage, but we kill each other in a stylized way so the audience is not actually worried. They see that the performers are alive and well and they're going to get up and go home.

Drunkenness or being stoned on drugs is practiced with sense memory, if you've ever been drunk or stoned. If you haven't, you've observed drunk people and seen that they have trouble with

balance, as they feel dizzy. Their speech may be slurred. They're often trying to act sober. A word of caution: Use these altered states
sparingly and don't be so "drunk" or "stoned" that you cannot be
understood.

"SICK" OR "INJURED"

Also, it's not a good idea to begin a scene playing "sick" or "in-
jured." Though injury or sickness may happen in a scene, we need
the piece to be about relationships (i.e., the mother is in need of
care and the daughter doesn't want to take care of her).

MANTRAS FOR SCENES

Tweaked from K. Johnstone

This is an exercise to give your mind something to do to leave less
mental space for preplanning or worrying. It also creates a specific
mood at the top of the scene. Before going onstage, choose one
of these phrases to tell yourself silently: "I love you." "I hate you."
"I'm curious about you." "I need you." "I'm scared of you." Keep the
words in the back of your head, repeated like a mantra. You will
not speak the phrases out loud at all. You may switch to another
phrase that starts with "I" and refers to a feeling, want or need,
whenever the piece calls for a change. When you are fully engaged
and concentrated on the piece, you will not need the mantra and
will likely drop it or forget it, as you'll be responding to your partner organically. You can revisit the mantra anytime you need it.

RHYTHM AND REPETITION IN DIALOGUE
Intermediate / Advanced. 2-3 players, standing or sitting.

This technique helps improvisers become more conscious of
rhythm and musicality in language. I sometimes bring in poetry
and have the actors read it silently to themselves and then aloud to
the group before doing this.

For example: you say to your partner, "I'll tell you a story about my
family that you haven't heard before." Your partner repeats back
to you, "A story about your family?" using language that was con-

tained in what you said. If someone asks a question, "Well, what's going on with you?" You might reply, "What's going on with me?" And then you answer the question. Incorporate something that's been said, and then add your own new text. Let's just start with this—I'll give you a word for a prompt: "Surprise." You're going to talk to your partner and say something like:

"My god, I got this letter and I'm so surprised because it's from him."

And she's going to say back to you, incorporating something you said:

"From him?"

And then go forward. You want to sense the rhythm and musicality in the language. Repetition helps with that. It's not that you're going to do this with every dialogue exchange in a scene, but you'll have the option to do it in certain circumstances, when you need time in a scene to get established and to connect, when you find yourself rushing, and when you work with musical accompaniment. Subtext, how you deliver the line, really comes into play here.

Demo with Joya and student:

Joya: You want to know what I think of this? I'll tell you what I think of this. I think it sucks.

Student: Sucks? Well, a lot of things suck.

Joya: Yeah, they do, but this sucks in a particular way. This sucks in a way that is going to lose money.

Student: Well, money sucks.

Joya: Money sucks. I could have guessed you'd say that.

So it's a bit like poetry. It begins using language in a more conscious way. Try this with two or three different partners. Then try it while getting up and down or walking together or moving continuously. Explore the timing: how quickly or slowly you respond to you partner, when and how long you pause between words or phrases.

THE VOICE

Though many exercises in this book involve body and voice, the ones below focus more specifically on the voice as instrument.

BREATHING FOR THEATRICAL SPEECH OR SINGING

Breathing for vocal production is different than meditation or yoga breathing, in which you may breathe in and out through your nose or in through your nose and out your mouth. When you are speaking, in performance or singing, you will draw in the breath quickly through your mouth when needed to support your sound, looking for opportunities to take in air in the pauses between words. You can get more air, quicker, inhaling through your mouth. There is no speech or song without breath.

VOCAL SLIDE, A VOICE WARM-UP

Begin by breathing in, through the mouth, filling the lungs with air. Then release a prolonged AHH sound that slides from your highest pitch, as though dropping over a waterfall, down to your lowest pitch. Think of the high pitch as coming from the top of your head and the low pitch from the bottom of your pelvic bowl.

Do this several times from top to bottom and from bottom to top. Keep your eyes at eye level as your voice moves up and down.

SOUND MASSAGE (FROM *AN ACROBAT OF THE HEART*, WITH A FEW CHANGES)
Intermediate / Advanced, pairs

Standing, one person begins by finding the most open sound that comes from her body with the least effort, a relaxed sigh. Her partner/coach touches the back and chest of the sounding person to find where the vibration is the strongest. (Of course, you will find the strongest vibrations in the throat, but we are looking for resonation here, not the source of the sound.)

Then the coach moves her touch from the starting point while the sounding person allows herself to respond to the touch with sound.

As the coach moves her touch slowly across the sounding person's chest, over the shoulders, across the back, up over the head, then along the arms and so on, the sounding person simply allows the pitch, the vowel sounds, and the placement of the sound to slide, as if in answer to the touch. At each place, the coach feels for the vibration answering her touch. If she finds a place where the sound does not vibrate, she may change the quality of her touch by pressing harder or more softly or by moving in another direction.

It often helps for the touching person to ask periodically, "How does that feel?" Then, in answer, the other partner may use sound or words. If you make eye contact while this happens, you can facilitate the discovery of the emotional content of the vibration.

After working the upper body in a standing position, have the vocalizing partner lie down while you work with the legs. There is no need to push the sound into places it does not wish to go. Many people find that as they allow the vibration to enter the abdomen, they begin to laugh. If that happens, don't fight it; let the laughter happen. But go gently; if a great deal of emotion or laughter happens, don't try to go any further. Your body needs to take time to become used to the new vibrations it is experiencing. Then switch roles.

VOCAL VARIETY AND FLEXIBILITY, ISOLATING ELEMENTS OF THE VOICE
Intermediate / Advanced. In a circle.

Working with the elements of vocal variety:

- Volume

- Pitch

- Tempo/Rhythm

- Duration (the length of each syllable and silences)

- Articulation

- Tone, emotional color ("Don't talk to me in that tone of voice.")

Each student tells us something about his life in the last day or so, not worrying about the content at all. The point of concentration is vocal variety, exploring the elements listed above. No need to "make sense." Just think of expanding the range of your voice. Move as much or as little as you need to. You don't have to think about what you say. Just spew and enjoy. We'll go around the circle and each will have a one-minute solo.

All but the most experienced students find this revelatory. They often don't realized how much variety of sound they can make. This exercise will help performers use their voices as instruments, to carry meaning and to encourage musicality in speech. This exercise will need to be repeated often, as speech patterns are very ingrained and habitual.

BACK-TO-BACK SOUNDSCAPE
Intermediate / Advanced, pairs

Actors stand back-to-back, touching each other's backs, but not leaning. They close their eyes and each takes a few seconds to find their own center. Then, beginning with breath sounds, one of them makes the first offer. Each responds to sound with sound. Beginning simply, they let the density and complexity of the sound evolve organically. They will keep their feet planted, but be free to move the upper body in any way triggered by their impulses. They are exploring musicality and extending their vocal range. Through stimulus/response they discover how the voice carries feeling in "conversation."

As the sounds develop, they may add words while keeping the focus on the sounds the words are made of. Since the eyes are closed, concentration on listening and hearing is acute. Players may find this exercise to be "trippy," a bit intoxicating. (Yes!) At some point the leader may direct them to open their eyes and see if they can keep their auditory awareness very alive. If they're keeping the soundscape strong, they may release the back-to-back position and turn front or to face one another. Ask them to negotiate a closure to the piece they've created.

VOICE LADDER
Intermediate / Advanced, pairs

We start with a vocal slide, letting the voice drop from high pitch to low with an "uh" sound, like steps, like scales. Your partner is going to say, "There," at a certain pitch and you'll stop there. And that's the pitch you're going to speak in. Play with that pitch and see if that pitch reminds you of someone, brings an image to mind, perhaps of a character. Find whatever the voice is, explore it. See if you can move into some kind of transformation. How does that voice affect your posture, your gestures? How does it feel in your body, especially your face, head and chest? Of course, no one speaks in exactly the same pitch all the time, so really, this pitch is just the "home base" of this voice. Notice where the voice is in your body so that you can revisit it. Notice if talking that way makes you move differently than usual; perhaps unfamiliar gestures emerge. And then your partner will have a turn. You'll have two voices each. Then we'll witness each other playing with your favorite of those voices.

SONG CIRCLE/RHYTHM JAM
Intermediate / Advanced. In a circle.

One person (an improviser or the director) offers a brief, easy-to-repeat, sound phrase without words, like La La La Da Da Pop or Hey, Hey da da da. It can be almost any sounds. It's the rhythm and melody that matter. Players are reminded to listen and respond, to sense when it's best to lay out or to soften their volume to serve the whole piece. Suggest that players mark the rhythm with their bodies: bouncing, tapping feet, slapping themselves, or snapping fingers.

Next, the whole group, along with the leader, repeats the phrase in unison. Then the next player in the circle creates the same process, until all have offered a new phrase. No one is to interrupt. The next player takes over at the end of the phrase, on the beat.

It's good to have the director, or someone in the ensemble with a strong sense of rhythm, playing a percussion instrument like a shaker, drum or tambourine.

Then settle on one rhythmic riff and have the ensemble sing it. Taking turns around the circle, each player will sing (or talk rhythmically) a little solo. A few words or phrases in rhythm, while the group acts as background singers using the simple sounds of the last riff.

After all have had a turn to solo, the leader moves the ensemble into a jam in which words from the solos are drawn upon for lyrics. The rhythm is kept throughout. If the group relaxes into it, this is usually quite intoxicating.

I teach my intermediate/advanced ongoing students a simple song, which we sing as part of our warm-up, not to learn to be singers but as part of our acting training. We sing it out together and solo, adding a variety of emotional life to the delivery. Choose a song you can sing in a round.

Many people have heavy judgments about their singing ability, so we confront that anxiety and look for the joy in song. We sing for inspiration, pleasure, and release, and to strengthen our voice.

CONTENT / STORYTELLING

Remember that all is in motion, is growing, is you.
Remember that language comes from this.
Remember the dance that language is, that life is.
Remember.

—Joy Harjo, from Remember

Given the unscripted nature of improvised theatre, we need techniques that players can use to influence the content of their pieces, making it more likely that content will be meaningful and well written.

UNDERLINING

Ensemble or class members bring in photos, news articles, poems, personal stories, or objects to share with the group at the beginning of a session. I call this Underlining because we often underline relevant writing from magazines, newspapers, or the internet and bring the articles to class. This helps improvisers know what's important to their colleagues and is held by the entire ensemble. The material may be referred to in a piece and will help the players create a shared world.

Reviewing our life is one of the things we do as improvisers, preparing for performance. I like to have a cauldron of stories, images, and quotes bubbling in the back of my brain ready to be fished out and revealed when the moment calls for them. However, and this is key, in order for the content of any performance (or conversation in life) to be fresh, we must be unattached to sharing any particular material at any particular time. We must be willing to follow the energy of each moment and to trust that what needs to be said (or NOT said) will emerge organically out of the interaction of the people involved. This is a combination of preparation and spontaneity.

STORYTELLING / NARRATIVE ARC

We often tell stories directly to the audience, penetrating the fourth wall. As I work with my students to develop the skills of "writing on our feet," I request that they read and see as much theatre as they can. I also recommend reading short stories and memoir. I urge them to keep a journal and to make lists of stories from their lives.

As we work with actual experience from life (which can be really satisfying in solo), we need to craft our autobiographical material as we craft all material. When we use our own stories, the danger is that we're attached to saying it how we think it happened, even if it would be more artful to let the story go in a different direction. I find it helpful to think of all onstage, improvised "writing" as fiction, no matter what the source, in the way that a play is fiction. That attitude gives us some protection, and therefore, more freedom.

DIRECT ADDRESS

In a scene we often use direct address (as in Shakespearian "asides") for characters to speak their subtext or inner monologue to the audience. The other players in a piece act as though their characters cannot hear the direct address, but, of course, they try their best to hear everything. Direct address should be used to tell the audience something they do not already know. An actor who's been playing the son of an older actor says to the audience, "I know he looks like he's just a mean curmudgeon, but when he's sober he can be the nicest guy in the world."

When new students are asked to tell stories, many will be nervous about it. Remind them that they already know how to tell stories. They do it nearly every day, talking to people in their lives about what's happened to them. They see and read stories all the time—in movies, TV, short stories, novels.

The terms "narrative arc" or "story arc" refer to the chronological construction of plot in a story. The information below contains a textbook definition of an arc, but I usually explain it in a way that seems more applicable to improvisational acting, like this: "The characters are introduced, and as the piece progresses we begin to understand what they want or need (their objectives). Then the story of the piece is created by the action of the characters trying to get what they want. Remember, objectives change in response to the unfolding reality of the piece. There are obstacles in the way of characters getting what they want and the action is how the characters deal with those obstacles. The piece is usually (but not always) concluded when an arc with a beginning, middle, and end has been created and the questions of the piece have been answered. Examples: Will these people reconcile or will they separate? Will the world come to an end? Sometimes these questions are left for the audience to answer in their own imagination. I'm most satisfied when the style and shape of the pieces are more elliptical than linear, yet has an underpinning of a narrative arc."

TEXTBOOK DEFINITION OF NARRATIVE ARC

A narrative arc is made up of the following elements: exposition, rising action, climax, falling action and resolution.

Exposition: The introduction to the story in which characters are introduced, setting is revealed.

Rising Action: A series of events that complicate matters for the protagonist, creating a rise in the story's suspense or tension.

Climax: The point of greatest tension in the story and the turning point in the narrative arc from rising action to falling action.

Falling Action: After the climax, the unfolding of events in a story's plot and the release of tension leading toward the resolution.

Resolution: The end of the story, typically, in which the problems of the story and of the protagonists are resolved. This is traditional storytelling. It's really good to know how to do it and great to break the rules and let the story be as nonlinear or poetic as it wants to be.

STORYTELLING EXERCISES AND STRUCTURES FOR ENSEMBLE

(See SOLO for more storytelling structures)

TWO-OR-THREE-WORDS-PER-PERSON STORIES, BEGINNERS

With beginners, you can warm up for collaborative storytelling by having students tell a story in the circle using only two, then three words each. Players should say their words immediately after the person before them, without taking time to think. I usually have folks say "Period" when they want to end a sentence, but all other punctuation is assumed. The writing need not be linear or logical but should make sense grammatically. It shouldn't be "who then going was" (unless you want to sound like the poet, E.E. Cummings).

PASS THE STORY OR GIVE-AND-TAKE STORYTELLING, THREE VERSIONS
3-5 players

VERSION 1: PASS THE STORY

In this collaborative storytelling structure, the tellers, standing facing the audience, each contribute to the ongoing writing of the narrative. Before they begin, the teacher may give each player one word that they must use in their first installment. Ask students in the audience to contribute these words, which can be drawn from categories, such as emotions, relationships, places in the world, body parts, "isms" (Socialism, Buddhism, Darwinism, etc.), or the word can be something that concerns or inspires or surprises them. This gives the tellers a bit of structure, which may serve as content prompts.

One player volunteers to start the story and then others chime in on impulse in this way: players may either interrupt their partner in mid-sentence and take the story forward or the teller may pause mid-sentence, indicating that she wants to pass the story on. For absolute beginners, it's easier to go sequentially, picking up the story from the person next to you and passing it down the line. Or, requiring more alertness, let the order of telling be random, with players jumping in when they choose.

Place one player in the center of the standing circle. He is the receiver of the monologue. The speakers, who assume they are one person, speaking from one point of view, are talking to him. Passing the monologue around the circle, one person at a time contributes his installment by either interrupting his partner in mid-sentence, or the teller may pause, passing on the monologue to his neighbor as in Pass The Story. When interrupting, the player is listening for a time when their neighbor's contribution feels complete (usually 20-60 seconds per person). The leader may start the ball rolling by delivering the first lines to the person in the center.

Example: "I'm so sorry to tell you this. It's so hard for me to say, but I don't think I can come here anymore. The thing is..."

The receiver in the center responds nonverbally and shifts his position to see each speaker. The character of both the speaker and the receiver will emerge as the monologue progresses, as will the relationship and situation. You can also try this with every other person in the circle communicating without words, with emotional and physical life only, to advance the monologue. When finished, all share what they noticed.

VERSION 3: INNER LIFE, COLOR, ADVANCE (ADD TO PASS THE STORY)

For a story to be evocative and dramatic it usually needs to contain these elements:

- Language that vividly describes what is seen, heard and smelled; the outer world.
- The protagonist's (usually the teller's) inner life; what he's thinking and feeling.
- A plot: what happens, the characters' progression through the world of the story.

There are also effective forms of performance that have little or no plot, such as a portrait of a person who is significant to the teller or a philosophical ramble, which can be rich and beautiful.

To practice, we can break down these elements and assign three improvisers to each take responsibility for one of them.

- One can specialize in inner life.
- One can specialize in outer life (to "color," painting pictures with words).
- One can be responsible for advancing the plot.

At first the teacher may direct the students, calling out "color," "inner life," or "advance" as the story progresses. Then, at a certain point, the students can direct themselves, jumping in, interrupting each other, with their contribution to the story. Of course, when storytellers have internalized writing technique, they will all have the responsibility and joy of including all elements. Also, suggest improvisers "keep it simple" by not introducing too many characters or storylines. Encourage them to explore each idea or image before offering new ones.

REINCORPORATION

When players have become comfortable with basic storytelling, tell them about reincorporating (also known as callbacks). This refers to reusing something: language, movement, or props that were introduced earlier in a scene or story or show. This technique helps to integrate elements of a piece or of a whole show. Anton Chekhov's maxim says it well: "If a gun is revealed in act one, it should go off by act three." People enjoy the click of recognition when they hear or see material they are familiar with.

TWO-MINUTE LIFE STORY WITH PARTNER

The group is spread around the space, in pairs. A tells her life story to B, who listens attentively. The leader times this at 2 minutes and gives a 10-second warning for closure. Then it's B's turn to tell. Since the time is short, each teller must make choices as to what material to include. This process reveals what is emerging as important to each teller at the moment. The leader should encourage all to notice how much editing or censoring they are doing. Editing may come out of a need for safety or privacy. That's fine. Or it may be a thought like, "You've had such a boring life," which is a heavy judgment.

After both have finished, they move on to new partners and again tell their tales. This time they are asked to tell different stories, though still using material only from their own life. This can be done a number of times, as folks won't run out of material.

INTERCUT STORIES
Intermediate / Advanced

This is a performance structure that can be done with three or four actors. I prefer three, as it gives each storyteller plenty of time.

The actors, lined up laterally, facing the audience, start by one of them asking the audience for a theme: "What concerns or inspires you?" They may get two suggestions they like and may choose to work with both. The storytellers will take turns telling (parts of) their stories, all of which will respond to the given theme(s), though each story is autonomous and intended to be quite different from the others.

Each player will be interrupted several times by his colleagues and will relinquish the focus when that happens. Who tells first is determined by who has the first impulse. For their first installment, each player should have at least 45 seconds to establish his narrative. After that, the tellers may interrupt each other at shorter intervals, making sure to vary the length of each person's turn. We want to orchestrate the intercutting, being very aware of musicality and timing. Some bits of story may be as short as 5 or 6 seconds, some as long as a minute. Each time an improviser interrupts, he will incorporate one or more words into his story that the previous teller has said. When a player is interrupted mid-sentence he may continue speaking for a few words to complete his thought. It's fine if two people are briefly speaking simultaneously.

Example: In teller number one's story she says: "Though I've been in this country for twenty years, I still feel like an outsider." The next speaker might include in his story: "I'd been in this country only a few days when..." Or: "I could tell that he felt like an outsider." Or "This went on for twenty years." These stolen words should come early on in each installment.

In order for each actor to be able to focus on creating her own story, she must listen to her partners with about 10–15% of her concentration, not letting herself get involved in others' stories, only sensing a good time to interrupt. This may seem difficult to do, but most of us, in everyday conversation, often listen with divided attention, experiencing images and thoughts associated with what we're hearing and thinking about what we'll say when it's our turn to speak. Consciously directing our listening is an important exercise in concentration. It makes us feel very awake and alert.

So, what about physical life? What are the improvisers doing when they're speaking? And, more challenging, what are they doing when their partners are speaking? There are several ways to handle this.

Tellers are encouraged to gesture freely and move as much or as little as creative instinct demands. When actors are not speaking they are in the world of their own narrative, visualizing the setting and radiating the atmosphere and emotional life of their story.

Here are some possibilities for physical life/composition:

At the top, all players begin with back to audience, turn front when they speak, stay close to their starting spot and turn back again when interrupted. In this style, non-speakers stand still but not "frozen."

Or, all face front at the top, step forward and move freely about while speaking. And improvisers may move when not talking as long as they do not pull focus from the teller. It's fun to experiment with style, searching for what most pleases your ensemble. This structure could even be done with players seated in chairs, getting up and down as needed.

A whole Intercut Stories piece may take 9-20 minutes (3-7 minutes per story), possibly longer with four players. To craft the shape of the piece and help to find an ending, it's good if the actors and director agree ahead of time about how long each story will be. Each player must sense when the stories are coming to a close and begin listening to their partners a little more. Then, one player at a time will end. Sometimes, one story needs more time than the others, in which case the performer will take time at the end to finish his tale.

INTERCUT STORIES INTO SCENES
Advanced

Intercut Stories may also transform into a scene which includes all players (an advanced technique.) This is initiated by one player breaking into his partner's world by speaking directly to him. For example, teller A speaks to the actor next to him: "I'm surprised that you're an immigrant, your English is perfect." If this happens, all players dissolve the imaginary walls they've erected between them and are now all in the same world. Then the ensemble proceeds to create a scene with all the usual, necessary interaction. Players already know something about each character from having heard bits of all their stories. Sometimes one player will choose to stand outside of the group and create a direct address commentary on the action of the ensemble.

These techniques require lots of skill, but are very interesting to do and to watch. The transformation always surprises the audience. I recommend only breaking into a scene with improvisers who have worked together a lot and who have agreed to do it ahead of time.

SPOKEN WORD MUSIC
Advanced

A performance structure for two or three actors and musical accompaniment. The musician plays a percussion instrument, keeping a steady beat.

Actors stand close enough to touch with the musician about six to ten feet away. Again, the performers may ask for a theme word or two from the audience. They will collaborate in creating a story or a philosophical riff in rhythmic speech, keeping in time with the musician. Performers move in rhythm and/or mark the beat by slapping their bodies or tapping their feet. A strong sense of rhythm is required so that bodies can be on "automatic pilot" and the actors are free to concentrate on language and orchestrating the piece. Though this is not a singing piece, the actors may throw in bits of singing. Sometimes one or two improvisers will act as a chorus, making sounds or singing to accompany their partner's language. Sometimes two of them will talk simultaneously. The idea is to tell a story with beginning, middle, and end while staying in rhythm, similar to rapping. This structure requires big listening, flexible voices, musicality and lots of practice. There is a video link on my web site of a performance of this form.

MIRROR STORIES, A BEAT BEHIND
Advanced

A performance structure for two actors, this one is very difficult to explain unless you have seen or heard the comic duo Carl and Carl on TV or the radio. I looked on YouTube to no avail for a video of them. However, I did hear a tape of them recently on KALW, a Bay Area public radio station. There is a video link on my website of a performance of this form.

Actors stand shoulder to shoulder and collaboratively tell a story, or dispense information, in this way: one of them begins by offering the first line of a story. #2 repeats the line a beat or two behind and offers new language, which is then echoed and mangled by #1. Again, sometimes the two of them will talk simultaneously or interrupt each other. The success of the piece relies on good timing, playfulness and intuition.

WHAT KIND OF CONTENT CAN IMPROVISATIONAL THEATRE SUPPORT?

In a two-person scene in an advanced FSI class, I stopped the actors after Rachel (in response to her partner saying "It's been a long time") collapsed to the floor saying that her child had been killed in a plane crash. A heaviness came over the scene. Her partner looked confused and, as an audience member, I felt uncomfortable.

In-class discussion

Joya: What brought you to that, Rachel? That offer that your daughter was killed. Do you know why?

Rachel: Oh yeah, 'cause I'm working with the loss of my kid.

Joya: You mean that she's living with her other parent, right?

Rachel: Yeah, she's alive, she's fine. She just doesn't want to talk to me, like forever. I wanted to up the stakes really big. I wanted to see what would happen if I went really big. I tried to think of the worst things. Plane crash...I just wanted to take it far.

Joya: Yes, the loss of a child is probably the worst thing that could happen to you. Imagining that would certainly create an emotional charge. As an acting tool, you could use it in certain circumstances. You could use that image if, for example, you had to cry on cue. But that would be in a situation where a play would require that kind of feeling and the play would justify it. When you go into something like that, a real tragedy, the piece itself has to earn it or it won't ring true. So, this brings up the issue of what content improvisational theatre can support, what it can carry. I'm glad it came up. What works in a solo may not work in a scene. In my opinion, even in dramatic ensemble improvisation, if it's not your own experience, it's really hard to earn the inclusion of this kind of tragedy. In dramatherapy, yes, you might explore the feeling of loss in that way. But I don't think it fits within improvisational performance. We're not doing Greek tragedy or Shakespeare. This form is much more informal, much smaller scale. You don't have enough control of the writing. And more important, in an improvised scene, there's the problem that this kind of offer is difficult for your partner. If I were your partner, I probably would not want to go there with you. It's really hard to use something that heavy, with that kind of pathos. Your partner could do a creative block to shift the content and say something like, "Oh sweetheart, you haven't taken your meds. Having bad dreams again?" But it would be better not to put your partner in that position.

Michael (Rachel's scene partner): You probably noticed I kind of froze when Rachel said that. I didn't know what to do.

Joya: Yeah, I noticed. Really what you want to sense for as much as possible is: what does the piece need? If you go into a scene with the agenda "I want to see what happens if I offer some really big, tragic material," that takes you out of the moment, away from just responding to your partner, out of the organic flow of the piece. Now, in class, you can do or say almost anything, as long as it's not harmful to others. It's class. We're here to explore. But onstage, it's another thing.

A few years ago when one of my actors in Lucky Dog Theatre performed in an Intercut Story with two other players he started his story being on a train and then back and forth through increments of the story it ended up the train is going to Auschwitz. His partners' stories were of a much lighter nature and I think the audience was confused about the tone of the whole piece. I don't think you can deal with Auschwitz respectfully in improvisation. It just doesn't work. Performers do write pieces about their own horrific tragedies. I directed one, a solo about the performer's loss of her son. But this was her real experience, and the content was carefully written. Of course, there are comedians and playwrights who use cancer, war, racism, all kinds of very serious material in their writing and it works, can be powerful and theatrical and even funny. As some of you know, I wrote and performed a solo that was partly about my husband's cancer, really about my response to taking care of him. Of course you can use the truth.

But this loss didn't happen to you, Rachel, and your partner may not know that. Your daughter isn't dead; she just doesn't talk to you. That reality you can use. It could be very fruitful material.

The audience in improvisation has a different mindset than in a scripted play. They likely know or suspect that in FSI much of the material may come from the performer's life. You don't want them to worry about the performer, though they may worry about the characters.

SOLO IMPROVISATION

You once were wild here. Don't let them tame you.

—*Isadora Duncan*

olo improvisational performance is significantly different from ensemble performance in that the actor has the option to use known material: stories from life, bits from written work, moments from previous improvisations, and still call it improvised (or semi-improvised) if it hasn't been performed before exactly as it is and won't be in the future. As there are no other players to help craft the piece, no partners whose reality she must embrace, it can develop in the unique style of the soloist, with content and movement that is compelling to her.

SAFE IN VULNERABILITY

Over many years of listening to adult students' personal stories, it's clear to me that many functioning folks struggle with extreme shyness, depression, anxiety, phobias, obsessive/compulsive behaviors and the frequent presence of rage and fear. I've been saddened to witness revealing stories of chaotic or brutal childhoods. Students in my Solo Performance workshops or in a Full Spectrum Improvisation class will often reveal issues in their lives. I'm proud to say that the non-judgmental atmosphere in an FSI workshop encourages vulnerability. We can learn to feel safe in a vulnerable state. If we allow it, we will find healing in the release of an open heart, body and mind.

Performers who are willing to take the risk can go for the thrill of stepping on stage alone, clear as water, empty as a blank page, ready to use whatever impulses come. You can start with no pre-determined content, stepping out and attending very closely to what's happening with your body/mind. What's catching your attention? How does the atmosphere in the room and the previous events, affect your choices?

PRESENCE

We need to develop presence on stage in all performance, but it's especially important in solo performance. It's a function of concentration, energy and commitment to the moment.

In beginning Full Spectrum Improvisation classes, students practice briefly standing in front of the group and allowing themselves to feel the supportive energy being radiated from their fellow students. Some enjoy it. For some, being witnessed may be uncomfortable at first, but confronting that discomfort is part of this training. It helps to think of the audience as a group of trusted friends. The teacher may suggest that the students allow movement impulses to be expressed and that they experiment with radiating energy back to the group. They can also be given a task, such as to count how many people are wearing black.

After they've been witnessed for 30–45 seconds, I ask students to report the experience, noticing how different tasks affected them. Then I work with them in response to what they reveal.

PRESENCE / DISAPPEARING / RADIATING
Intermediate / Advanced

Being able to radiate energy is an important skill for any performer. An actor stands at the edge of the playing space "offstage," then steps on to the "stage" and feels the more intense and electric energy there. She finds the place in the space in which she feels most powerful (this takes 15 seconds or less) and comes to stillness there facing the audience. She checks into herself, and to her central axis, which connects her to the heavens and the earth. She feels her feet on the floor, long spine, chest open—and connects with her personal power. Then she radiates this energy outward in all directions. She finds a feeling of ease. The awareness training and character work she's done should aid in this task.

The actor may move as long as the movement or gesture is truly needed and felt. She must monitor her mind/body to notice if her thoughts leave the room and, if that happens, bring her awareness back to this present place. When she's ready (after at least 30 seconds), she may release her concentration and shift focus to the next task, which is to "disappear." For this she will withdraw her presence (energy) from the room. She may change her body position and not look at the witnesses. Each actor will find their own way of doing this. It's always fascinating to watch both tasks. Again, when she's ready she can "come back" to here and now.

INNER PROCESS

What happens in an improvised solo? What is it made of and what does it look like? How do you start? A solo may be language/narrative based or movement based or start one way and evolve into another. If it's language based, we still want it to be embodied.

See if you can let your body determine your beginning by moving on to the playing space (stage) in exactly the way your body wants to. You need not understand this impulse. Just follow it. Of course, this would work as well as an offer in a duo.

Two Examples:

Example #1

When it's time to start my solo, I drop to my hands and knees on the floor at the edge of the playing space. I'm scared but also excited. I crawl toward the center and begin to speak as I rise. Being on the floor has reminded me of an incident from my childhood, so I start telling the story of being with my friend, Nancy, on the floor of the basement playroom of our house on Long Island. We're 8-9 years old and we're playing doctor. I'm the naked "unconscious" patient whom Dr. Nancy is examining.

In performance, I don't question the impulse to tell this story, in which my mother catches us in sexual exploration and sends Nancy home saying she is not welcome in our house ever again. The feeling of shame surrounding this incident leads me to other movement impulses and more childhood stories, which are somewhat fictionalized memories.

Example #2

Here's a transcription of part of the text and a description of the actions from another solo I did recently. This piece was

MICHAEL ASTRAUSKAS

accompanied by the violinist, Yehudit, whose playing was sparse, but very evocative and full of feeling.

I walk over to the stacking upholstered chairs that are stored at the edge of the space. I pick one up and carry it onto the playing area. As I put it down I notice that it's heavier than I thought and I look at the audience and say:

"I like to sit down now more than I used to, now that I'm older." As I say that, I remember a video I saw on TV and I tell the audience about it.

"Someone did a documentary about old people who live alone. There were these people in their 80s, some in their 90s—who were interviewed about being alone. I watched four or five interviews. There were women and men, sitting in chairs talking about how lonely they are. Just terribly lonely."

As I'm talking, I'm pushing the chair around and leaning on it as though it is a walker.

"And they all said just how much they love being in their own houses, how they were so attached to their homes, to their own things, the familiar furniture and bedspread and photographs. But it was so empty and so quiet. A thin, white-haired woman mentioned coming home from shopping and coming into the house and there was almost an echo, it was so empty. When she sat reading or watching television, she would talk to her husband sitting next to her in the empty chair—her husband who had been dead for twenty years. When she was watching, she'd remark to him about the program on TV."

Now I'm picking up the chair and moving it to another space and sitting down in it and getting up from it in various ways intended to show my body stiffening with age.

I say, "Maybe they can all live together in a big house and be less lonely." Then I find myself talking more about our attachment to our homes.

"I've lived in my house for 25 years. My mother-in-law lived in this house for more than 50 years—hardly able to imagine another place that could be home. My husband and I moved in after she died."

And as I'm saying that, I find myself near the wall and I look at the wall and I say, "All these walls have memories. These walls have eyes and ears." And then I put my ear to the wall and I listen and I say:

"If you listen to the wall in your home, you might hear the voices of the past the way you hear the ocean when you put a shell up to your ear. You might hear the voices of your children or grandchildren. Or the children you never had."

This little bit triggers a brief series of movements and miming a shell to my ear. And then back to walking the chair as a walker and more text. The whole piece took about seven minutes.

WHAT SHOULD I DO WITH MY EYES?

In solo performance classes I'm often asked, "What should I do with my eyes? Where should I look?" There are options. The performer may look directly at the witnesses, making eye contact very briefly with each person (this is often done in traditional storytelling). Or she may look slightly above the viewers' heads or slightly to the side of each face. This will read as though she's looking directly at them. As a solo performer, that's what I do. I don't actually look at anyone's face as I find it distracting. When I'm in the audience, I want to be anonymous. I don't want the performer's eyes on me for more than a few seconds. I suggest that the actor experiment with looking out both ways. When you're on stage you often can't see the faces of the audience because the theatre lights are in your eyes but (in direct address) we look out at them as though we can see their faces. In intimate and informal venues, we sometimes are quite close to the audience and can see everyone in the first two or three rows. And of course, in class, you can see all your classmates as you deliver your solo.

FACT IN FICTION

Most effective solo improvisations I've seen contain a core, or at least shards, of personal history or observation. A word about mixing memoir with fiction: It doesn't actually matter, artistically, if an event really happened. Our memories are notoriously unreliable anyway. It may matter psychologically. The question is how we deal with the feelings it arouses and how we shape and deliver the material.

I once took a week-long workshop led by a psychologist called "Re-Writing Your Life Narrative," in which we told the story of our childhood looking for valuable learning and investigating our past from the point of view of a wise and loving adult. In my story, the many times I felt I didn't fit in with my peers in school or social life, I began to see as the birth of the artist in me. The therapeutic value of transforming one's life experience into art is obvious. I've felt it myself and seen over and over with my students how empowering this process can be.

That said, there are times when we feel compelled to stick to the "truth" whether or not it's the most fruitful creative choice. Students have often told me that they feel it's being dishonest to mix "fact" and fiction. To help free us from this constraint try these exercises:

STORIES WITH GIVEN PHRASES: MIX MEMORY AND FICTION

One improviser gives another two lines to learn by heart. Then each tells a story including the two lines they were given. The class will guess which were the known lines. You can also have slips of paper available on which to write the lines and give the papers to performers as the solo or scene is in progress. The players may integrate the given material at any time, not necessarily the moment it's given.

BRIEF REPORT OF THE WEEK SOLO
INTERMEDIATE / ADVANCED

Usually about 60–90 seconds

Going around the standing circle, players tell something that recently happened to them. Keep the story embodied as well as being attentive to creative and varied use of the voice. Tell us about your life and include something that did not happen. It's fruitful to go around the circle more than once.

SPEWING AND MOVING CONTINUOUSLY

Having two tasks at once creates a level of concentration that often has no room for the editor, so the language that emerges is often more original than what is "written" while standing still or sitting.

We're focusing on spontaneity and release. What needs to be expressed? Start with any movement and keep moving no matter what, as you speak continuously with no concern for the content. Keep talking and moving for a whole minute. (Leader cues player when time is up.) Move slowly or quickly. If there is still energy in your impulse after a minute and you want to go further, that's fine. You can have thirty seconds more, or another minute. Just spew.

You can also start with given language, such as "I feel..." and free associate. It doesn't have to make sense. It could be "I feel like a woodpecker and want to go to bed..." See if you can just open the channel between your brain and your tongue and let it rip without editing.

TWO-MINUTE SOLO: RANT / CELEBRATE

The solo starts out as a rant, a big complaint, something that's important to you. Kvetch. Then, after around 60 seconds, you're going to let the rant transform into a celebration of the same issue. You'll shift your attitude about the issue. It can be a sudden realization or a gradual shift. Both points of view are presented with conviction.

GIVEN MOVEMENT QUALITIES / KNOWN TEXT

Improvisers move through space embodying movement qualities given by the director, such as: expansive, contracted, flowing, flying, staccato, sensual, released, languid, heavy, or a combination of two qualities, i.e.: sensual/released, blocked energy/jittery. As players move, they deliver a short bit (4–8 sentences or phrases) of known text, letting the movement influence the tone of the delivery. Do this two or three times with different movement qualities each time and the same text. This can also be done with improvised (discovered) words, noticing how the movement generates text.

EXPERT SPEECHES

A short speech or lecture delivered by an "expert" about a given subject; something you know nothing about. Make it up. We're not looking for facts here. The teacher gives the prompt. Examples: animal husbandry, robot mechanics, Romanian history, taxation in 19th-century Italy, String Theory… Players use full gestures and as much or as little movement as needed.

THREE CLAPS

A solo exercise that's fundamentally about impulse and practicing freeing yourself from the inner editor. It can be done with two claps if you're short of time.

One at a time, a student gets up on stage and turns her back to the audience, standing there for about five seconds just finding her center line, relaxing, breathing. And then at a certain point the teacher is going to clap, hard. When the actor hears that clap, she'll turn around and express what is happening in that moment; any impulse in the form of movement, language, singing, any form that we've been using in class. She can just stand there and look at us if that's what she wants. The point is allowing the impulse to be expressed fully and without judgment.

She'll do that until finished with that action. It can take five seconds or 90 seconds. When she feels that the behavior is complete, she'll turn around, with back to the audience, and return to centered neutral. Then the teacher will know the actor is ready for the second impulse and she'll clap again. The player will turn around and do something else. It might be a continuation or development of the first impulse or some behavior that is completely different. Again, when finished, she'll turn her back to the audience, return to centered neutral and then there'll be a third clap. We don't critique these performances; this is just practicing enacting impulses.

ROUND ROBIN TWO- OR-THREE-MINUTE SOLOS

Each player gets up and tells a story, with the content or theme triggered by performers who went before. Improvisers sitting in a lateral line in the audience get up sequentially. The teacher gives the first teller a word prompt.

LIVING SCULPTURE SOLO
Intermediate / Advanced

Two people: one to perform, one to prepare.

This structure is for class and performance. After a brief demonstration, a player in the ensemble, or even an audience member, will sculpt one actor into a transformed shape, including the actor's face. The receiver thinks of herself as clay and holds the given shape. The solo actor will then feel into the new body shape noticing how this shape creates mood and age and explores how to move from this place. Images will arise for the actor, triggering impulses for speech. I ask her to introduce herself to us, imagining us as sympathetic strangers.

She'll discover a character inhabiting this new body. After exploring how this new entity moves, the actor will sense for what that being has to say. What voice emerges? Through this exercise, you can discover characters (and their stories) who later became the core of new scripted solo pieces or characters who may appear in an improvisation.

For scenes:

Four persons, two statues and two sculptors, the sculptors design their statues then leave them on stage. Slowly the statues come alive and start a piece, triggered by the initial posture.

NO-TOUCH SCULPTING

One actor shapes the other by moving his hands a few inches from his partner's body, as is done in Living Sculpture, but without touching his partner at all. The receiver responds as though touched, using sense memory to feel the contact.

CHARACTER FROM WORST TRAITS SOLO
Intermediate / Advanced

This structure invariably creates surprising and revealing pieces, often filled with dark humor.

Actors are asked to think of a character trait in themselves that they strongly dislike, that they consider a flaw. Then each does a solo (3-10 minutes) in which they let that aspect of themselves dominate the personality of the character on stage. There is great relief in this action when performers discover that their severe self-judgments are rich fodder for performance.

Example: A young man tells us that his girlfriend complains that he is emotionally unexpressive. He tells us this in a tight, repressed voice, looking uncomfortable, eyes averted. As his story progresses, he exaggerates the character's inhibitions, saying that his girlfriend wants to talk about "sexual activity." He can hardly get the word "sexual" out. He goes into a scientific speech in which he tells us: "All mammals procreate and humans are mammals." His body is squirming peculiarly throughout. He concludes by telling us that he's working on relaxing, and he does some very funny breathing and eccentric movement to demonstrate relaxation.

He's delighted with his performance, as are we. The character he's developed is touching and engaging and can be brought to life in his later improvisations.

CHARACTER FROM BEST TRAITS SOLO

This is another version of the exercise above, which, not surprisingly, turns out to often be less juicy than the Worst Traits one. However, if the "good" traits are exaggerated and explored, they can also be engaging and compelling. **Example:** An older woman tells us how generous she is and offers to cook meals and give massages to everyone in the room. As she continues talking about how happy it makes her to take care of people, she begins to cry and eventually segues into an angry rant about how people take advantage of her. She also reports having enjoyed her performance and says it was cathartic.

TELL YOUR PARTNER'S STORY

Pairs to prep, solo to perform.

Actor A tells actor B an autobiographical story. Then B tells A his story. Each story may take 3-6 minutes to tell, depending on available class time. The actors are to listen attentively, visualizing the setting of their partner's story and allowing themselves to imagine the events of the narrative happening to them. Then each actor will tell the story to the audience as though it is his own history. The process of making a character's reality your own is essentially what actors do with a script.

Tellers should be coached to portray, as accurately as they can, the emotional and narrative essence of the received experience. As imagination training, however, it's a good idea to allow tellers to add details that they didn't necessarily hear from their partner. Often these additions turn out to be close to some unspoken events of the story.

It's often easier for actors to partner with someone of the same gender, as life experience is affected by gender.

SING TO INVISIBLE OTHER
Advanced

A solo acting exercise that requires singing. Each actor is asked to recall a song, or part of a song, about 8-12 lines, that they know well. It should be a song that evokes emotion in them. The actor gets up onstage and sings the song three times.

First, to the audience, to explore and enjoy how it feels to sing this song.

Second, the actor "materializes" either his mother or his father; that is, he visualizes his parent to one side of the audience and sings the song to her or him.

Third, the actor materializes a person in his life with whom he has undelivered communication and sings to that person. Performers should take time to really see the absent person in the room. This exercise tends to stimulate deep feeling rather quickly. Somehow, singing moves us in ways that speech does not.

SIT AND WRITE
Intermediate / Advanced

We do solos from language prompts. For advanced workshops or performing troupes you may sometimes want to sit and write together during a practice or class break. I often do non-movement activities after lunch during a full day workshop and during multi-day intensives. Here are a few suggestions to use for spontaneous writing and for improvised solo stories:

"Today my name is…" "What I really want to say is…" "My mother's hands…" "I have to go…" "I remember…" "I don't remember…" "My father's voice…" or themes such as "Rivals," "Forgiveness." Make up your own.

You can start your piece with these words or use them as a trigger for images and/or memories to arise in your imagination. I've known many improvisers who do not write, but who create artful and strikingly original text in practice and in performance. Still, the act of writing helps to connect improvisers to the part of the brain that creates language. It's fruitful to get up after writing, shake your body out and verbally improvise another monologue from a fresh prompt.

During a practice session with colleagues in which we focused on language, we used the prompt "I am from..." The following was my piece, written in eight minutes.

> I am from a faraway dark place where people wear heavy coats against the bitter cold and speak a language that only their countrymen and women understand, that is not spoken anywhere else in the world because many of the words have a bitter angry undertone, like music in a minor key or like the growls of an aggressive dog. And I am also from a warm, colorful place where the people wear white cotton and red silk and finely-made leather shoes and love to dance and sing and eat together and talk with a lively melody in a tongue no one but their own people speak but that is spoken in other places in the world by members of this tribe who live in English-speaking and Hebrew-speaking and Turkish-speaking and Spanish-speaking countries. And I am from America, that great homogenized conglomerate sprawl of industry and electricity and cornfields and roads, where land pulsates and jumps and slinks and covers itself in asphalt, loud music, and the sound of automobiles revving up. And I am from a tiny sub-tribe, a skittering flock of dancing beings who often cry out in pain and pleasure and whose faces are stripped bare by huge grins and are shiny with tears.

(The first two places I'm from refer to Russia, my mother's place of birth, and my father's heritage as a Sephardic [Spanish] Jew.)

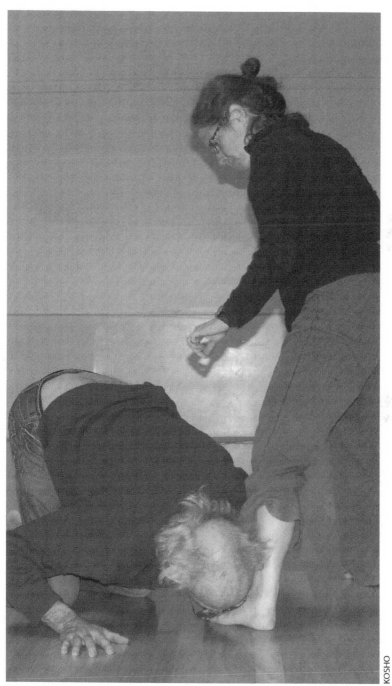

CONCEPTS, PRINCIPLES, IDEAS, SUGGESTIONS...

Never let the gods be absent from your stage.

—*Mary Austin*

HOW DO YOU KNOW A PERFORMANCE HAS WORKED, WATCHING IT OR PERFORMING?

These answers came out of discussion with my colleague, Owen Walker.

- A transformation happens, some sort of event in which both the audience and the players are altered. There is a sense of discovery.

- The audience and the players are entertained and/or inspired.

- There is congruence and integration of form and content and they support each other.

- The performers radiate a feeling of ease and vitality.

- There is an unbroken line of present awareness: passion, engagement, commitment, beauty, imagination, momentum.

- The piece contains meaning, points of view or questions about real life.

SUGGESTIONS FOR PERFORMERS

NOT SO FAST

- In Full Spectrum Improvisation we usually start scenes with physical and emotional life only. Although sound is welcome at any time, performers are asked to postpone speaking until they've taken time to connect with themselves and their partners, discover the atmosphere of the piece and sense for the relationship between their characters. This may take 10 seconds or a minute. Or more. Though in many improv classes students are taught to define all, or most, of the given circumstances: who (relationships), what, where, when (possibly objectives, also) within the first 30 seconds of the piece, I strongly recommend against it. I think this is taught as a way for improvisers to feel secure, to have predictability. Unpredictability is one of the joys of improvisation. Strong technique will bring security onstage. In FSI "where" and "when" are often not verbally defined at all. If performers feel that the imagined physical environment is important to a piece, they can define it through behavior: looking at "the sky," shivering from "the cold."

- If they are engaged, the audience will enjoy interpreting the story for themselves. You don't need to spell out every detail.

- Endowing another actor with a specific identity at the top of the piece can put the named actor in an awkward position. In the interests of authenticity, it's best to let the character endowments emerge organically and collaboratively over time as the actors observe each other and their connections develop. Often defining the characters verbally is not necessary. Naming them doesn't always deepen meaning.

- The most engaging and satisfying improvised theatre pieces (to watch, as well as to create) are born from impulses that come from the immediate realities of the players and the energetic exchange between them. This includes the performers' memories, dreams and fantasies.

- Avoid using actors' real names on stage unless you are breaking the frame. It tends to take players out of the imaginary world they are creating.

BEING HERE

- Mostly keep the action on stage; avoid talking a lot about people or things that are not there, unless it's your husband who your friend (she's here) is having an affair with. Or something like that. Be sparing about introducing new locales like "Let's go to the hospital," which will force you to focus on creating a new "where" instead of sensing for what needs to happen next between you and your partner. I notice that these "Let's go somewhere" offers often come

when players are attempting to logically fix problems the characters are having. We don't want trouble fixed until it's escalated enough for us to discover something in it. And we don't need logic.

DEVELOP EACH BEAT

Often, when improvisers are feeling insecure in performance they will jump from offer to offer, as though just offering more material will save the scene. Believe me, it won't. Because the players have no faith in what they're doing, they're judging each offer as not good enough. We want to train ourselves to notice when we're doing this so that we can slow down and connect with ourselves and our partners. We need to develop each beat before moving on to the next one. Use techniques such as joining and physical actions that express what you're feeling or what you need (like hugging your partner). Also, use Repetition, Breaking the Frame, Direct Address....

STORIES AWAITING

Often when we are playing in an improvised scene, story ideas and images come to us. We can sometimes keep these storylines in waiting in the back of our minds while the piece unfolds. As we stay present listening and responding to our partners, we look for a place to fit these ideas into the world of the piece. How pleasurable it can be when the idea you've been harboring can be expressed and embraced by your partners and clicks into place like the missing piece of the jigsaw puzzle. Other times, we find we must let go of the story we're carrying and let a different, collective story be born.

THAT WAS GREAT. WHAT WAS IT?

If you ask an improviser after a show what she remembers, she'll often say she doesn't remember much (though memory does vary greatly from person to person). With the most engaging pieces, we remember less than the ones which didn't work so well, because we're not in the logical mind. We're "in the groove," in an altered state, driven by instinct more than thought. We're in control and letting go of control. However, there's much to learn from every performance (and there may be material you want to use in a scripted piece) so I recommend writing what you do remember in your journal as soon as possible. You can also ask colleagues, the director, or friends in the audience what they saw.

FREE ASSOCIATION HAS NO REINS

In a heightened state of concentration, the ability to free associate is enhanced. If we allow free association free rein, it can provide us with endless material. Some improvisers think there is a danger of the associations being too "familiar" or "obvious," but if they are personal to each player they'll be weighted with meaning. Certain images, themes and characters will emerge and recur again and again because they resonate in our life. It's not fruitful to try to avoid this.

STATEMENTS VS. QUESTIONS

In dialogue, statements are often stronger offers, but questions are welcome as long as they don't put your partner in the position of having to define something you are avoiding defining. In other words, try not to put your partner on the spot.

PERSONAL HISTORY / HERSTORY

For the most part, it's juicier if players assume that the characters know each other and that there's a back story which will be revealed in time. If the characters have some personal history together, the possibilities are richer and the stakes will be higher when there's trouble in the relationship. That said, comedy pieces often work well when the characters are strangers. And in a three-person scene, there's a nice tension if two of the characters know each other and the third is a stranger to one or both of them, as in my scene with Martin and Owen in the introduction to this book.

HOW LONG?

Scenes (or pieces, as I like to call them) or solos may run from 3-60 minutes. We want to find the length that each piece needs, letting the event have the space and time it requires.

IDEA AND IMPULSE

> *Nothing great in the world*
> *has been accomplished without passion.*
>
> —*George Hegel*

A DISCUSSION OF THE DIFFERENCE BETWEEN AN IDEA AND AN IMPULSE

Here are some dictionary definitions:

Idea: Something merely imagined. The mental image of something known. An intention. A plan of action. A thought. A conception. A plan or design according to which something is constructed.

Sounds like ideas are useful for writing stories (on your feet or not).

MICHAEL ASTRAUSKAS

Impulse: A sudden inclination to act without premeditation. Momentum. Impetus. An application of sudden force causing motion. Force caused by some external stimulus.

Throughout this book I celebrate the creative power of impulse and instinct. I don't mean to imply that in life we should act out whatever impulses arise. Of course not. As socialized adults we need impulse control. But in some people the necessity for self-control (and their personal history) has had the effect of limiting or shutting down self-connection, so that the person can't quite identify what she feels or wants or what behavior is authentic for her. It's my hope that FSI training can create self-awareness that allows for choice. In improvisation we make choices every moment and we need to have access to all feelings and impulses in order to be able to choose which to act on.

From the definition above, we understand that impulses refer to the psychophysical world. They are the fundamental action of improvisation. And yet, we need the intellect to create content that is rich with meaningful ideas. So we work with both forces: impulse and idea, intuition and intellect (lots of I words). Both sides of the brain are active, creating a feeling of full engagement and aliveness. But we need to let intuition lead. If we are always, or almost always, aware of our senses, our ideas can be born in the body.

In other words, let our impulses lead to our ideas in theatre, most of the time. Not always. Sometimes we have subject matter that we deeply want to work with. This is often the case, and works well, in solo improvisation. It can work in ensemble, especially if the group spends time together talking about what matters to each person.

THE INNER DIRECTOR VS. THE INNER CRITIC

As we internalize technique, our inner director can support us in making aesthetic choices. The inner director notices the stage picture, reminds us to make eye contact with our partners when needed, suggests varying our vocal volume or tempo, reminds us to develop that movement riff.

BEGINNINGS AND ENDINGS

A philosophy always comes after a technique.
Do you walk home with your legs or your ideas?

—*Jerzy Grotowski*

BEGINNINGS

At the top we need to be as receptive and alert as possible. Atmosphere is particularly important. We need to sense for it, clarify it, be guided by it. And, of course, we need to connect with our partners to find our way to a felt beginning. Sometimes a player will speak at the very beginning of the piece before all performers are in connection. When that happens the players may be off to a tricky start.

During practice, let yourselves stop and restart if you feel you've made an inauthentic beginning. Please, do not continue with a behavior that feels wrong. You don't want to practice false acting. You can call out to your partners "Restart, please," and take this opportunity to talk together briefly about why you stopped the scene.

In class, if I feel the actors are not in connection with themselves or each other I'll often stop them and ask how it's going. I want to know the actors' experience before I share my observation because that knowledge will guide my comments. If they feel it's going well (and I don't think so) or one player is happy, the other's not, that needs exploring. When I'm interrupting a piece I try to be as brief as possible so the players can get back to playing quickly. Sometimes it's best for them to start a new scene, applying the feedback they just received.

When side coaching at the top of a piece, I may say: "Let us hear your breathing." The sound of the breath communicates emotional states and helps to establish atmosphere. It helps the actor clarify, intensify, and radiate his feeling state. I once saw a TV interview with Marlon Brando in which he said, "Acting is all in the breathing." Of course, he said other stuff about acting, too.

In practice and performance, try starting with some version of Reflect, Extend, Respond or Silent Tension and maybe add a mental mantra (see Mantras for Scenes in Chapter Five). Also, joining with your partner's behavior can be very connecting. All pieces contain the attitude of Let Your Partner Change You. Beginnings are different for improvised solos. See the section on Solo for thoughts about that.

Example: Beginning. I frantically run onstage, then off again, then on. As I move, I'm tracking my partner but not looking at her directly. She's moving too, slowly. We make eye contact and then she speaks. I stop in my tracks, looking at her. We're launched. I feel that I've begun the piece with a strong connection to my inner reality and to my partner. I feel at home on the stage.

ENDINGS

If there's a narrative arc of any kind in the piece, all players will be following it to some degree and will have a sense of when the story is coming to a close. At that point no one will offer new beats and all will be letting the energy of the piece settle, sensing for closure. The scene might end in an embrace or a handshake or a waltz. Or you may end with alienation. You might not get together at the end. You might go off with "Fuck you."

Players may create a quick, sharp ending. There may be unanswered questions re relationships between characters and the events that have occurred. We don't need to tie up each piece neatly in a bow.

If the piece is more abstract and nonlinear, the arc will be energetic rather than literary. Try this for practicing endings: if a player feels strongly that the end has arrived, but is not sure all are with her, she can call out "End" while going to stillness. All would then come to stillness in a tableau. You won't usually do the calling out in performance, just in practice, unless you're breaking the frame because the piece really needs to end. There are times when, in spite of being skillful, improvisers just can't find their groove. All know the scene isn't working, and likely is not going to work. It's painful. In this case it's a good idea to end it and get off stage.

You can end in a freeze frame or in motion while exiting the stage, or one or more players can exit, leaving someone behind to end alone on stage, a nice opportunity for a brief solo.

I like the technique of having one scene segue into the next with only a brief beat in between, with one or more of the players staying on stage for the next piece. Movement and/or music can serve as a transition between pieces.

If the show has performances of different forms—solo, direct address stories, ensemble scenes, etc.—you can clump two or three of the scenes together. Attention should be given to the overall feel of the show, with players reincorporating themes and/or images towards the end of the show that emerged at the beginning.

In comedy improv the lighting person or players who are not in the scene often decide when the piece ends by turning off the lights or by using a gesture, which they call "editing," to signal endings. All players are expected to heed this signal and drop the scene immediately. Or, as in the short form game-based TV improv show Whose Line Is It Anyway? the host hits a loud buzzer (EEK!), ending with a joke or a laugh line. We don't do that in FSI as it takes away the actor/writer's control over their work. The exception would be if the lights are being run by the troupe's director or she's signaling the lighting person or the players that the piece needs to come to a close. A slow fade can give the players 10–20 seconds or so to find an ending.

If you can track and feel the emotional progression of the relationships, and the changes within each character, the ending will likely find you and your partners. You don't need to remember every bit of information that has been revealed during the piece.

NO HAROLDS IN FSI

When I was studying improv at The Committee and other places, we learned the popular form called the Harold, which is done with five to a dozen players coming and going, often very quickly, in and out of the scenes. It starts with a word suggested by the audience. The opening scene or monologues establish the story and theme for the rest of the show. Then separate scenes and/or monologues are created that contain the characters introduced early on and introduce new ones. These scenes are presented in any order, moving forward or backward in narrative time and are interwoven to make a cohesive narrative (or not) by the end. Often players are tagged out and replaced by another improviser who plays a new character. This form requires remembering myriad characters, information and story lines, which grow more complicated as the piece develops.

Though I sometimes had fun doing the Harold, I often had a hard time remembering and following all the frantic and language-heavy activity and found myself thinking, thinking, thinking, trying to figure it out, my logical mind working overtime. I would often feel drained and unhappy after doing one of these improvisations. Needless to say, the Harold was not the form for me.

Though I've seen Harolds done brilliantly and found it very entertaining, I've seen this form more often produce thin, conventional stories, devoid of real feeling or meaning, performances that seem mostly devoted to fulfilling the rules of the game. I've thought about why this is. Players can find movement possibilities in a Harold but there is little opportunity for self-revelation or personal discovery in this form.

Here's a *New York Times* article that helps explain how holding a lot of information in our minds affects creativity. I want to acknowledge that when acting in scripted plays, we are required to remember pages and pages of text. But acting from a script is an interpretive art, not a generative one, so, aside from our acting choices, there's no need to make things up.

THINK LESS, THINK BIGGER by Moshe Bar

I discovered how much we overlook, not just about the world, but also about the full potential of our inner life, when our mind is cluttered. In a study published in this month's *Psychological Science* the graduate student Shira Barror and I demonstrate the capacity for original and creative thinking is markedly stymied by stray thoughts, obsessive ruminations and other forms of "mental load." Many psychologists assume that the mind, left to its own devices, is inclined to follow a well-worn path of familiar associations. But our findings suggest that innovative thinking, not routine ideation, is our default cognitive mode when our minds are clear.

In a series of experiments, we gave participants a free-association task while simultaneously taxing their mental capacity to different degrees. In one experiment, for example, we asked half the participants to keep in mind a string of seven digits, and the other half to remember just two digits. While the participants maintained these strings in working memory, they were given a word (e.g., shoe) and asked to respond as quickly as possible with the first word that came to mind (e.g., sock).

We found that a high mental load consistently diminished the originality and creativity of the response: Participants with seven digits to recall resorted to the most statistically common responses (e.g., white/black), whereas participants with two digits gave less typical, more varied pairings (e.g. white/cloud).

In another experiment, we found that longer response times were correlated with less diverse response, ruling out the possibility that participants with low mental loads simply took more time to generate an interesting response. Rather, it seems that with a high mental load, you need more time to generate even a conventional thought. These experiments suggest that the mind's natural tendency is to explore and to favor novelty, but when occupied it looks for the most familiar and inevitably least interesting solution.

ACTING AND CHARACTER

Always act in your own person, as an artist. You should never allow yourself any exception to the rule of using your own feelings. When you are on the stage you must play yourself. But it will be an infinite variety of combinations of objectives and circumstances, which have been smelted in the furnace of your emotion memory.

—*Constantin Stanislavski*

dvanced classes are focused on performance skills. Improvisers who study at an advanced level generally intend to perform publicly. I've often asked my advanced improvisation students if they've taken acting classes, and I was initially surprised to find that many had not. I asked other improv teachers and found the same was true for their students. So it's necessary to incorporate acting exercises into classes. Students expect to learn acting through improvisation and, to a large degree, they can. Acting technique is a part of many exercises in FSI. Of course, there is technique involved in acting text written by someone other than the actor. For that, students need to work with scripts. For serious students, I always recommend taking additional acting classes as well as dance and voice.

ACTING EXERCISES: OBJECTIVES

The concept of objectives comes from Method Acting, from Stanislavski, and it's based on a lot of good psychology. Stanislavski was friends with Pavlov and researched other early 20th-century psychologists, so there are a lot of sound psychological principles about how to connect with real emotion and how the human psyche works. That's why Method Acting is so popular. Before Stanislavski, there was no acting training that would help anybody be natural. If you look at silent movies, the acting was very stilted because actors were taught a codified method where if you felt happy, you did a particular gesture; If you felt your heart was broken, another gesture. And everybody did the same thing, every character. It was not at all natural. So the Stanislavski System was a profoundly innovative training. There are many books out about the Stanislavski Method if you want to read about it in depth.

A student complains that the word "objective" throws her off. It feels analytical to her.

Objective just means, "What do I want or need?" That's all it is. So, you can also use the term: needs or wants. You can say, "What action should I take to meet my needs?" If any of the language bothers you, don't use it. How you think and the language you choose really matters—in art and in life. You can say, "point of view of the character" or "the character's values." See if you can find what works for you. If you find a word that is shutting you down instead of opening you up, change the language. We want, as much as possible, to be released and open and inspired. If there's a rule or a concept that's ever shutting you down, think about why that is and feel free to replace or abandon it.

WANTS AND NEEDS

Objectives are what the character wants or needs at any given moment. It is based on the idea that in life we always want or need something. We might not be aware of it and we might not have a good strategy to get it, but we always want or need something.

An action is what is done to move towards getting what is wanted, pursuing the objective. Because improvising actors will need to play a variety of roles spontaneously, they want to be able to construct characters quickly with physicality, voice changes, accents or other techniques as demanded by their instincts in the fictional situation. This requires skill. We practice character motivations because they are acting skills, but they are very tricky in improvisation. You can enter a scene with an objective that can propel you at the top—but as the piece progresses you have to let that objective be changed by your partner's behavior. You are always being affected by your partner, always responding to her offers. (How many times have I said that in this book?!)

DON'T BE ATTACHED TO YOUR OBJECTIVES

You have to let the objectives go when the piece calls for a new beat. You can't think them out ahead. It's not like a play where you can analyze each exchange and write down the objectives as you go through the script. The playwright has put the objectives in there; you just have to find them. But in improvisation, the play is not yet written. It's still out in the stratosphere. The beats are continuously changing. If you're back there in your first beat—your first objective—you're not going to be collaborating to progress the piece. If you think back on your scenes, you'll realize that objectives, that is, wants and needs, usually arise without your thinking about them.

There are other acting techniques such as the Trigger Technique, which holds that sometimes the character is trying to get something and sometimes they're just responding to what's just happened the moment before, which is a different thing. They're just responding. When I studied Trigger, I thought, "That kind of works better for improvisation than thinking that you always want something." Because a lot of times, in real life, people respond with actions that will not meet their needs. Both can be true: you want something and you're just reacting in the moment. The reality is that if improvisers are "in the groove," they will respond in both of these ways onstage because it's natural behavior. We study acting technique so that we have tools to expand our artistic possibilities when the muse is not with us.

A SIMPLE EXERCISE ON OBJECTIVES
Intermediate / Advanced, pairs

The objective will always be active: to do something. For example: to give her a piece of my mind, to comfort her, to seduce him, to get her excited, to persuade, to intimidate, to find a way out. How do you want to impact the other person? What do you want at this moment? Let's say the given objective is "To create excitement." You need to be specific, in your mind, about what that is about. To get your partner excited, think about something that is exciting that he might also find exciting. For example, maybe you bought a lottery ticket together and you won two million dollars. If that gets you excited maybe you'd pick that scenario.

Pick something specific and then speak to your partner about this thing. For the first round do this in gibberish or use the alphabet or numbers, so you're not concerned with creating text but only with emotional and physical life. Do this in a pure way, just dealing with emotion and not content, just pure feeling. I'll whisper the objective in the actor's ear so the receiver won't hear. After the actor is finished with his action the receiver will report truthfully what he received. Did the receiver feel excited? If not, what did he feel?

After the first round, you'll use English and say, for example, "Yowsa! We won the fucking lottery! YEAH! Two million dollars!

KOSHO

I don't believe it!" Next, we'll focus on vocal and verbal life. Your partner, who is receiving you, is going to have his eyes shut. So, you may be jumping all over, which is great—I encourage you to move and gesture, any way that you like, as much as you need to—but they are not going to see that. They are going to hear you and feel you. So your voice and energy need to carry the objective you are pursuing.

In a minute or so, I'll say, "Let it go," and then your partner will open her eyes and tell you what she got. Of course, we'll switch roles. And I'll give some other objectives. The receiver has his eyes closed. He can do whatever he wants, but he's not going to speak. He can respond emotionally. I hope he does.

After you're done, you're going to talk to each other about what was coming across. Spread out as much as you can, because you don't want to hear the other couples very much. If you are the actor, you can't touch—emotion has to be carried through your voice and your energy.

Then do a round where you pursue your objective with everything you've got: language and physical and emotional life. And, in the middle of playing with your partner, see if you can find a space to stop talking and just behave very physically, pursuing your objective without words. And make it really big, which, for excitement, probably wouldn't be very hard. Don't worry about it being naturalistic; just make it as intense and embodied as possible. Then you can go back to speech when you need to. I'll give you new objectives, and you'll switch partners.

SUPER OBJECTIVES

A super objective refers to the core needs and wants of any person. What do they want out of life? What's important to them? This, of course, tells you a lot about a character's values. What is her super objective? "To run the show?" "To make the world a better place?" "To amass power?" "To make her mark on the world?" "To be seen?"

That's who she is. Asking yourself this question can be a fascinating part of self-reflection. You'll likely find more than one super objective.

PRACTICING OBJECTIVES WITH KNOWN TEXT

Face-to-face with your partner, one of you is going to be the actor and one of you will be the receiver. Choose a sentence and pick an objective. Play the objective, with full physical life, then find a new one and use the same words. Try three or four different objectives with the same language then switch roles.

EMOTIONAL RECALL AND SENSE MEMORY

> *An actor, above all, must be a great understander,*
> *either by intuition, observation or both.*
>
> —*Sir Laurence Olivier*

In the Stanislavski Method, developing emotional recall and sense memory are taught as part of core technique. Actors practice remembering different emotional states they experienced at times in their life as a way to bring forth that emotion when needed. We must be specific in our conjuring up the details of each memory, visualizing and feeling the particulars of each moment: where were you when you felt excited (or scared or euphoric…)? Who was with you? Was it a warm day or raining? What were the sounds you were hearing? And most important, how did your body feel?

I've found that many improvisers connect with past feelings instinctively. For those who do not, practicing sense memory and emotional recall can help them have easier access to a broad range of emotional life.

GREETINGS WITH GIVEN RELATIONSHIPS
Beginner / Intermediate

Here's a fast-moving acting exercise that practices instant responses in encounters:

Improvisers form two lines, front to back, with the first actors in each line facing one another, at least twelve feet apart. The teacher calls out a kind of relationship and the first actors in each line move forward and greet each other within these relationships, i.e. long-lost friends, your former employer/employee, your mother, your child, your deceased grandma, your ex and so on. The actors will discover as they connect, who is the employer and who is the employee, who the mother, who the child. Or the relationship may be ambiguous but emotionally charged. There may be little language, or a lot, or none. They connect briefly (40-60 seconds) then move to the back of the line. The teacher then calls out the relationship to the next actors in front. When all have had their first encounter, switch the order of the lines so that the actors have a new partner with each new encounter.

FACE-TO-FACE FEELINGS
Pairs

Make eye contact and communicate different emotions to your partner just with your eyes and face: tenderness, sympathy, happiness, anger, fear, disgust, domination, sadness, etc.

MEMORY-IN-THE BODY EXERCISE / PSYCHIC TUNING
3 Players

Player #1: Recalls emotionally charged memory and puts her body in position associated with incident (i.e.: vigilantly waiting for someone, curled up on the floor hugging herself, smiling quietly, etc.). There can be small movements as well.

Player #2 is the director. She observes #1 and directs #3 into the same position.

Player #3: Assumes body position of #1 by following the directions of #2. When ready, #3 senses for and guesses the memory of #1. Students should not expect to guess exactly what #1 is feeling or remembering. They just need to be in the emotional "ballpark."

GLADIATORS: PUSHING / RESISTING
Pairs

A physically demanding exercise to release anger and passion. Actors should be about the same weight and not frail or fragile.

Two actors stand facing one another and imagine there is a line drawn on the floor a couple of feet behind each player. They take hold of each other's hands and push their partner backwards with the goal of making the partner step over the line. Have them release sound as they push and encourage them to use their full strength. It doesn't matter who "wins," that is, if anyone is pushed over the imaginary lines. The idea is to unblock psychophysical energy. They stop when either player needs to.

FACE MEMORY—MY VERSION AND EXTENSION OF AN EXERCISE FROM *AN ACROBAT OF THE HEART*

Intermediate / Advanced, pairs

Sit opposite your partner (either in a chair or on the floor), close enough to be able to touch her. Your partner sits looking at you, while you study her face. Take a couple of minutes to "learn" that face. Allow yourself to feel all the feelings you have as you do. Meanwhile your partner allows herself to smile or whatever; she doesn't need to be a statue.

When you have finished, your partner takes her turn "learning" your face. Then when both of you have finished you turn away so that you are both facing empty space. Now, in that space, try with your eyes and memory to discover that same face in the space in front of you. Take a couple of minutes to see if you can feel and see the face you just learned.

KOSHO

Then each of you go sit opposite a new partner and try again to discover the face of your first partner, but this time do so in the space directly in front of the new face. You're projecting the first partner's face onto the second partner. Try focusing a little above, below, or to the side of the face. Figure out what allows you to take in the real face while seeing the image at the same time. Most of my students find it easier to see the remembered face slightly to the side of the real face in front of them.

Then find a new partner and project a face of someone in your life (who is not in the studio) onto the face of your fellow actor. Choose a person you know well and who is, or has been, important to you. The important thing is not that you can actually hallucinate; it is to learn how you can use your eyes to perceive inner images even as you observe the outer world.

In improvisation, and acting in general, we often project an identity of a person not present on to the actor we're playing with. If our partner is playing our lover, we may endow him with the emotional charge we have for our actual lover.

It's well known that the ability to visualize varies greatly from person to person, so some actors will find this process difficult or impossible to do. We want the images to trigger emotion so it often works for those actors to project feelings, rather than images, about an absent other onto their improvisation partners.

KOSHO

The actor imagines with his body.
He cannot avoid gesturing or moving
without responding to his own internal images.

—*Michael Chekhov*

CHARACTER

Most character exercises are taught only in intermediate and advanced classes.

For the actor, connecting the body, voice, and imagination is essential. When I studied in the late 1970s with members of Jerzy

Grotowski's famed Polish Laboratory Theatre, we were taught that "Everything must come from and through the body." Grotowski believed that, "We do not possess memory; our entire body is memory and it is by means of the body memory that impulses are released." Michael Chekhov's famous book, *To the Actor*, contains many useful exercises, as well as theory, about physical acting. Stanislavski, in his later work, focused on physical actions to penetrate into the sphere of feelings.

Character transformation is physical transformation and we approach it by exploring the possibilities and endless variations of physical shape, gait, breathing, gesture, resonance of the voice.

Students tell me that they sometimes have this thought while in a scene: "My character would/would not do that." For example, "yell at her sister," "run around in a circle," "laugh at that joke." I ask, "How do you know what the character would do?" This thought comes from the logical mind yet actually makes no sense, as the characters in improvisation are not yet written, they've only just emerged. If the actor has a sense for what the actor/character wants, the actor's behavior will reveal what kind of person he is. With the influence of change in body and voice and a sense of objectives, the character would do what you want to do, feel what you feel at this moment. That said, we can develop characters in practice that may emerge later in the course of an improvised piece.

Students have criticized their own performance in character as being "not consistent." I ask: "Is consistency an interesting theatrical value?" "Is the behavior of real people consistent?" Also, what we mean by "character" in FSI is quite fluid. In FSI, we often create improvised pieces without playing a different age or gender at all. As I've said, we're in both the fictional world and the real theatre at the same time. We can drop a character at any time (Breaking the Frame) and comment on her. "Wow, that English accent is a bit slippery."

CREATING THE PHYSICAL LIFE OF A CHARACTER

Something uncanny, and perhaps even instinctual, happens
when we imagine the transformation of
our human selves into an animal nature.

—*Anna Halprin*

ENSEMBLE CHARACTER EXERCISE

Students have warmed up and are doing a natural, everyday walk around the studio while in a state of heightened sensory awareness. Teacher's narration below.

I want you to change the shape of your spine as you walk. What shape appeals to you at the moment? Change the shape of your spine a lot. Try a couple of different shapes—and (after a few minutes) settle on one. Now, how does that play through your body since the spine goes all the way up to the neck, to the level behind the ears? How does that affect how you hold your head? And what does that do to your arms and hands? What has changed? Is there a different tension now in your body from what there was when you were doing your own natural walk?

For some of you it's playing through your whole body, which is what we want, all the way down to your feet. Is there a change in your feet? A tightness in your hip joint perhaps? In the back, in the shoulders?

What animal would your character be? A mammal, bird, insect, reptile? Notice where your energy center is in your body. Is it in your head? Your chest? Your pelvis? Is it warm or cold, large or small, hard or soft? Try moving the center to another part and changing its nature to support your animal image. Do you feel emotionally altered? Do you feel younger or older than you are? Have a different image of yourself?

If you get a sense of who this might be as you're doing this, see if you can find a way to adjust this body shape so that it's doable and comfortable enough to maintain for five or six minutes. Some

body shapes just can't be sustained too long because they're just too physically challenging or painful. Explore this character's movement, sitting and getting up, walking slow and fast. Can you run? (If there is a full-length mirror in the studio, this would be a good time for the actors to look at themselves.)

Stay in this, we'll call it a character, and find yourself connecting with somebody else and see if you two can imagine that you're friends, and see if you can take a walk together, a leader/follower kind of walk together with this partner. How do you two adjust to each other's tempo?

If you feel the need to converse with your partner, you want to say something to her, tell her something about yourself or ask something, go ahead. What voice is coming out here? Explore.

Stop for a moment and release. Let that body go. Shake it out. Take a little break and then turn to your partner, one of you behind the other, and give your partner a shoulder massage. If she wants you to rub her back, do that too. Just receive. Don't help your partner.

Then switch.

Then, on your own, see if you can re-inhabit the character body you just released. Find it again and move around for a minute or so. Remember the image of the animal associated with this person.

PLAYING CROSS-GENDER CHARACTERS AND CHARACTERS OF A DIFFERENT AGE

In Viola Spolin's *Improvisation for the Theater* you will find exercises addressing character age and type. I won't repeat them here.

In improvisation shows one often sees actors playing a different age than themselves, or a man playing a woman, or a woman playing a man. Unfortunately, this is often done with little to no skill. I recently saw a comedy improv show in which a young woman in an all-female troupe said to another player, "Well, I'm your father so you have to listen to me." She needed to say who she was because her body and voice did not in any way radiate a change in gender or age. She looked and sounded exactly the same as she had in the previous scene when she played, basically, herself. So, sorry, I suggest that if you've not acquired the skill to transform to the opposite gender, don't do it in front of a paying audience. Work on it in class and practice.

Remember: age and gender are only a part of character. If you feel the need in improvisation to play a 90-year-old person, that person has particular characteristics and objectives in life, some related to his age, some not. Same for gender. Try not to confuse physical condition or mood with character. You need a good artistic reason to pretend to be very old or very young or to play a person of the opposite sex.

Here are some simple tips:

AGE

Joints become stiffer with age. There is often pain in the body. Many older people tend to move cautiously for fear of falling.

Young children are usually looser and more flexible than adults. They rarely stand still, preferring to skip, run, jump, fidget...etc.

Try turning your toes in slightly, arching your back a little and opening your eyes wide. And, of course, you'll need to pitch your voice higher. Yes, this image is a bit clichéd but it does indicate childhood and makes you feel altered.

CROSS-GENDER
FEMALES PLAYING MALES

For a woman to read as a man or a man as a woman, without the aid of makeup and full costume, exaggeration is required; character transformation will be broad. You may want to wear a piece of clothing to help with the transformation.

Men's voices are pitched lower that women's, so women actors must drop their pitch and men must raise theirs. Women's center of gravity is lower than men's because we generally have more weight and strength in the pelvis and they have more in the upper body. Women, try imagining that your arms are very muscular and hold them more away from your sides. Men have stuff between their legs that we don't have. Though not all men do this, female actors should walk with thighs more open and sit with legs apart.

MALES PLAYING FEMALES

Think light on your feet. Women weigh less. Try more flexibility and movement in the pelvis. Sit with your legs crossed or together. Let your hands be delicate and expressive.

MORE ON PLAYING SOMEONE DIFFERENT FROM YOURSELF

- You can play with your repertoire of characters in practice, developing your bag of tricks. Find out what your body can do and what is behind that character, what is it in you that corresponds with him? Why do you want to go there? Do you love him? Are you afraid of him? What is it about this character that is meaningful to you? Use your intuition and instincts more than analysis. Take an attitude of experimentation.

- Work on creating characters that are easily accessible to you so you can quickly step into a character when needed. Practice using your body, your voice and your status to make characters that are unique to you.

- What element(s) of nature would she be? Choose: cloud, fire, darkness, sunlight, thunder, wind, water (ocean, lake, river), volcano?

- Voice: pitch, tempo, tone, volume. From where in body does it resonate? A dialect / accent?

- What is her habitual tempo?

- Michael Chekhov's Psychological Gesture (PG) exercise: Using the main desire (super objective) of any character, create a whole body gesture that expresses this need. Begin with hands and arms, then include your whole body. You may find one or more PG's for different characters.

- Use observation. When you're in a cafe or at the bus stop or at a family gathering, even at work, notice how people walk, sit, stand, gesture. Are the feet turned out, turned in? What is the shape and tone of the spine? The shoulders? Are the hands relaxed? Of course, this changes depending on the context and mood of the person, but a certain pattern/shape remains.

IF IT HURTS, DON'T

Talking with a student after a piece in which the student held her body in a painful contortion.

Joya: How did that feel?

Barbara: It hurt.

Joya: I'll bet it did. That was quite a powerful bit but I was very happy you changed because I couldn't watch you for a long time. That's an interesting exploration, and if that did come up in a scene, you would need to get out of it rather quickly because in addition to it being torturous for your body, it would be hard for the audience to watch. If it hurts your body, after a while the audience is going to feel it.

If you find yourself in a position that physically you can't maintain or emotionally feels not right, there are ways out. (Fictional) drugs and alcohol are useful, magic wands are good, accidents, seizures are good ways to transform your character and stay in the fiction of the piece. You can give yourself an offer like this: "I see this pill over here....," a way to a transition.

Or you can break the frame and confess to the audience that you're in pain. Also, you can get off stage and come back as somebody else. "Oh, I have to go home to Mama now," or "I'm gonna go jump off the bridge." Go out, transform your body, and come back as somebody else. If you're in a three-person scene, you can stay out for a while. But whatever you do, don't stay in a shape if it's painful for you physically or emotionally. We don't want you suffering; we want you having a good time.

STATUS EXERCISES

In developing ideas for a show or a character, you don't have to hold onto what you think is a good idea. There are a million other ideas, don't hold out for a 'good' idea. Don't be clever. Work and play cooperatively with others and ideas will come in more abundance. Delight your partner. Slow down. Use less effort.

—*Keith Johnstone*

Keith Johnstone, author of *Impro*, an extraordinarily readable book, emphasizes the importance of being clear about each character's status. He says, "The statuses must change during the scene. If you know your status, you know what to do." For an in-depth investigation of status, see his book.

I teach some of his exercises (my variations) as technique for character and to heighten dramatic conflict in scenes. Status, if you think of it as power, exists in all relationships. The action of power/status shifts helps to propel the dramatic movement of our scenes.

Mostly, you do not have to think about status in your scenes. You know about it already. But, if the piece feels dull, you can use power plays intentionally to add fire. That's how technique works. You need it when the muse is not with you and you are not acting organically.

BASIC STATUS EXERCISE

I demonstrate how status is revealed through the body. "Everyone turn your toes inward, knees a bit bent. How do you feel? High or low status?" All reply "Low." Just that small physical change has created a change of status. "Now, collapse your chest and round the spine. Eyes are on the floor now, right?" I ask about status again. They answer: "Lower still." And some say "I feel depressed," "Feels like low self–esteem," "Oppressed." One way to think of these pos-

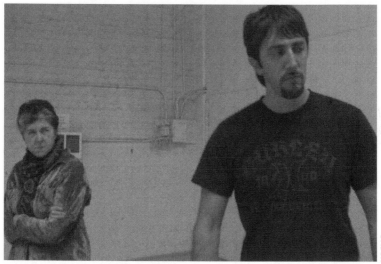

KOSHO

tures is that people in a low-status position or condition feel they have no right to take up much space. Their energy is pulled inward, rather than radiated outward, especially if they are afraid.

We try various postures and actions: feet way turned out, twitching, scratching, belching, darting eyes, limping (sad to say, sickness and old age are generally low-status conditions) I ask: "Do you feel like a different person now, not your usual persona?" All answer yes. "That's what we mean by character, right?" Then we try out high-status postures: "Lengthen the spine, open the chest and let your head be erect. Align your feet under your hips. Now look around, making eye contact with your colleagues. Walk smoothly, slowly and with ease. You might try a royal wave. How's your status, now?" All answer: High.

Then I ask the whole ensemble to imagine that they are at a company holiday party in the workplace. I give actors the given circumstances (who, what, where, when, relationships) sometimes for exercises but we never define them ahead of time in performance, as I want the improvisers to find those elements through their connection. But for some exercises it's useful to create clear focus on the technique we're working on.

I assign half the group to low status and half to high and ask them to mingle. I always enjoy seeing the variety of high-status executives: arrogant, mean, kindly and patronizing, threatening, sincerely generous. The low-status workers are terrified or confused or rebellious or dying to get out of there, or all of the above. Their posture and voices clearly radiate where they are on the power hierarchy. We practice this scenario for a few minutes, then switch roles. Then we release and shake out the characters.

Most of us feel "creeped out" being in either role. We talk about what happened and about how in real life we see people jockeying for status frequently. We do it ourselves. We live in a society where we're taught to measure ourselves and others in terms of "winners" and "losers," those who hold power and those who don't. We see that in healthy relationships power and status are fluid, passed around, always in flux. And, of course, with intimacy, power is shared, status struggles are abandoned, allowing vulnerability.

There's conversation about how this heightened awareness of status and power will affect us in real life. Certainly, we're reminded that how you carry your body profoundly affects how you are seen, and how you feel about yourself in life.

Then, working in pairs, we set up a scene with a given "where"—a public park, a museum, on the street. I avoid cafés or other places where characters are confined to chairs. The task of the scene is to compete with your partner for lower status. Each character has a need to be perceived as the most pathetic.

Players enter from opposite sides, off stage, and begin an interaction that is entirely nonverbal. They communicate entirely through physical life, breath and sound. I warn them to start with a fairly upright posture, so they have somewhere to go. By the end of the short scene both players are usually on the floor, possibly flat out, or on their knees. These scenes are invariably funny. Often, they're hysterically funny and painful, since comedy is based on human foibles. You can do the same exercise vying for higher status or having the players switch status roles during the scene.

After the nonverbal scenes, when we've felt status in the body, we do scenes that include language and we play with the high/low possibilities of status and power. Johnstone suggests that keeping one's status slightly above or below your partner's creates the most natural (certainly the most familiar) behavior. We do these scenes without setting up given circumstances. Letting the "what" and the "where" (if "where" is defined) arise organically out of the relationships.

I once taught an eight-hour Team Building workshop in Cincinnati for a group of Procter and Gamble product designers. They were supposed to be thinking up new coffee products and I was meant to help them be more creative. The woman who had hired me, a former student, had enjoyed status exercises in my class, so she asked me to include some in the workshop. I had some trepidation about the context but I did as she asked. The results were very interesting but not, I think, what the woman had expected.

At the end of the day as we were debriefing the workshop several of the workers said that the status exercises had heightened their awareness of the strongly hierarchical nature of the company they worked for and how it had affected their well-being for years. After class, two of the people told me that they were considering quitting. Doing the creative work we did together gave them an appetite to live a freer, more meaningful life. Needless to say, this was not what the company wanted from me. They didn't hire me again. Which was fine with me.

THE REAL THING
INTERMEDIATE / ADVANCED

The Real Thing is an acting "stretch" exercise; improvisations designed to explore a particular territory of challenging emotional life, specific to each actor. Example: Helen avoids acting aggressive or even authoritative on stage, so she is given the objective of dominating her partners' characters and playing high status. Or Sam, who rarely reveals vulnerability or gentleness, is given the objective "To reveal myself" or "To make everyone happy" or to play a lower-status character.

Often new actors play a similar character over and over because this behavior is habitual in their life. It can feel natural and easy for them. If this is a habit in real life, maybe it would be good to look for another role to play, as an acting and life stretch. I often see women playing caretaker roles, in which the story is about one character who is in trouble and the other is a caregiver character limited to one kind of action.

FULL SPECTRUM IMPROVISATION

PERFORMING ENSEMBLES

Logically, harmony must come from the heart... Harmony is very much based on trust. As soon as we use force, creates fear. Fear and trust cannot go together.

—Dalai Lama

The deepest ensemble work I've done or seen is by folks who've been together a long time and who nurture friendships outside of the studio. It's such a pleasure and so nourishing to work with people for whom we feel affection. Unity requires sensing the atmosphere and mood of the ensemble ("group mind") and working with this energy as you do with the space and content of your pieces. So, trust, in this case, means that each player trusts the others to make strong offers and to be present for receiving and developing offers. Players want to be able to rely on the skill and

NONIE KIMPITAK

support of their partners. We especially need these unifying factors because we have no script to unify us. There's a lot to learn through jams with strangers, but we should respect our art form enough to perform publicly only with people we've practiced with.

TAKING CARE OF THE GROUP

Internecine conflict happens to some degree in every group (in and out of the arts). It's human nature. It's how the conflict is handled that matters. Creating good theatre requires that actors make themselves emotionally accessible. It takes time and spaciousness to connect. The need for clear and compassionate communication among the players in an ensemble is an ongoing challenge. Students and professionals may become triggered or confused by a partner's behavior. We sometimes find ourselves needing to work out conflicts that arise during practice or performance. Occasionally someone will be triggered by another's offer. We hold authenticity as a high value, but we also need boundaries between our fictional and personal selves. Some people have clear boundaries.

Others' boundaries are very porous and they may take fictional insults as real. Sometimes I hear from an improviser after class or practice (often days later) that feelings of confusion, hurt or anger were triggered by their partner's offers, especially if the partner was playing anger, unkindness or rejection. Sexual or romantic offers can also be difficult. Offstage behavior may also trigger upset.

I use techniques of Nonviolent Communication, a conflict resolution and connection strategy developed by Marshall Rosenberg, which I studied for several years, to aid this process. I'm struck by Rosenberg's suggestion to "focus on the quality of the connection" rather than the content. Of course, students who are engaged in a quest for self-awareness and self-knowledge outside of class, work with their partners in class with more ease and harmony.

When someone is faced with a colleague that they don't particularly like, I suggest that they look for what they can like in that person. It can also be fruitful to explore what it is in the person that they are reacting to.

CLEANSING THE ATMOSPHERE

In class or practice, when a scene contains anger or fear or if it hasn't gone well, players can reassure each other after the piece that all is well between them by talking about it or by just hugging. The actors may want to "shake out" their bodies. I've also had folks do a little ritual action we call "Fluffing the Aura," in which one partner stands still and centered with eyes closed while their partner moves his hands in the air with a fluffing motion very close to, but not touching, the receiver. The idea is to "cleanse" away any residual bad feeling. Brief (one minute each) standing massages are also helpful. These small actions help to ease tensions and find release.

TOUCH

We want to be at ease with every possible action of the body, a challenging goal. The issue of being comfortable being touched by partners comes up every now and then. When it does, I ask the person to say more about it, to see if it's something we can deal with right then, or if it requires therapeutic support beyond the scope of class. Realistically, you can't do this work with any depth unless you're comfortable with body contact. Of course, we hold the expectation that we will treat each other's bodies with respect and care—avoiding touching breasts or crotches, taking care not to injure each other. It's essential that all improvisers feel safe together in class and onstage.

PERFORMING WITH LIVE MUSIC

I love working with an improvising musician who accompanies most pieces. A skilled musician can add artful complexity by extending and responding to the dramatic action and the rhythm and atmosphere of the piece. She provides a kind of sound track. I've found it works best if the musician mainly follows (and rarely leads) the actors, though she occasionally may offer a new feeling if she strongly senses it's needed. Or she may enter into a call-and-response game with an actor.

I've worked for years with Yehudit Lieberman, a virtuoso violinist, whose day job was playing with the San Francisco Ballet orchestra as well as having her own jazz band. She plays electric violin for us, which can make a huge range of sounds. We've also worked with cello and keyboard players and percussion, which I like for improvisation. Guitar doesn't work as well.

Having the group leader create rhythmic accompaniment in training or practice helps actors increase awareness of musicality. In class, those improvisers who want to try it practice simple percussion accompaniment for scenes. Sometimes there's a musician in the workshop who is happy to try out playing. This is not easy. It takes a lot of practice and skill to work with verbal life, to sense what to play, when to play, and when to lay out. The musician must be careful not to compete with the actors for the auditory space. There needs to be open dialogue between the director, the actors and the musician.

AUDIENCE INVOLVEMENT

Improvisational theatre can allow an interactive relationship with the audience. Improv groups frequently solicit suggestions from the audience as a source of inspiration, a way of getting the audience involved, and as a means of proving that the performance is not scripted. That charge is sometimes aimed at masters of the art, whose performances can seem so detailed that viewers suspect the scenes were rehearsed.

I'm actually very happy to improvise without asking the audience for input at all, but have found advantages to including them: we demonstrate that the material is actually made up on the spot, and we narrow down the myriad possibilities for content. When a player is flooded with impulses, suggestions can be a welcome help. We also create an informal atmosphere of inclusion.

JOYA CORY

The audience can be included in a number of ways. Here's a way I like: At the top of each show the MC can ask audience members to call out a word that represents something about which the person is concerned or inspired. Asking "What concerns or inspires you?" helps to guide audience members away from such words as artichoke or buffalo penis (words we've actually received before I devised a more specific audience request). Now we get suggestions, which are evocative to work with, like traffic, money, jealousy, climate change, food, love...

As there are usually several words offered, the MC picks the one or two she finds most interesting. The given words are used as a theme for Inter-Cut Stories or for scenes or solos. I recommend using audience suggestions lightly, with subtlety. If someone offers "traffic," your story may be about drug trafficking or an argument you had with your lover while driving in heavy traffic. You may not even utter the word "traffic," though it inspires your story. You may also want to try having audience members (in the first row of seats) pick out props from a basket at the top of the show and hand them to you before you start a scene. Of course, you are then compelled to make use of the given prop.

SPACE OBJECTS / MIME

The use of space objects and mime are an integral part of most comedy improv training. They can help to establish the characters in the "where." In FSI, I caution students against the frequent use of space objects because I find that when focusing on creating invisible objects, actors often are not focusing on the relationship with their partners. And, as a watcher, I often can't read the invisible objects/environment and am distracted trying to figure it out. If you're going to use space objects a lot, practice mime, develop skill.

Performers and students will often turn to space objects when the scene/piece is not going well. I've read this as a recommended action in several books about improv. It's not a good idea, as it takes the actors further away from real emotional connection with themselves and their partners. If a player really needs an object in a scene to create a reality that's important to her, she is free to mime it. If mime is used, the objects and actions should be easy to read and very informative about the character or story: i.e., smoking a cigarette, stuffing your mouth with food, digging a grave, putting on lipstick or makeup, guzzling from a bottle of booze, stabbing with a knife....

SPACE OBJECT EXERCISE

There's an invisible-object exercise I learned from Keith Johnstone that I've used fruitfully with beginners to stimulate the imagination.

One student gets up alone and is asked to go over to an imaginary closet (or shelf or bureau) and fetch the imaginary box that is there. He looks inside the box and pulls out what he sees. The student defines the size and shape of the box himself. As he looks in the box the teacher asks what is inside. Players can pick up an invisible book and read aloud from different pages. This helps students develop trust in their ability to make things up and to visualize invisible reality.

PLAYING WITH REAL PROPS AND COSTUMES

Real objects can serve as triggers for images, memories, and stories. Improvisers can assemble a collection of objects and costumes, grabbing something when it's needed during performance. In my basket I have two purses of very different styles, with a hankie in one and a sheet of paper in the other. I also have a bible, a jump rope (that's been used more than once as a noose and as a leash), an eggbeater, a deck of Tarot cards, a shrunken (fake) human skull, a tiny pillow. In my costume box I have a soldier's jacket, a lacy negligee, an old, nerdy-looking flannel robe, a sport coat, a trench coat, a black shawl, a purple feather boa, a long scarf, various caps.

I have wonderful memories of a series of improvised shows I did in the late1970s, in which we, the improvisers of MOTION, collaborated with visual artist, Jock Reynolds, to create physical theatre pieces in response to complex environments that Jock built in a large cement floored space. We entered the space, never having seen what he put there and discovered a new "set" and new objects each night—things like a bathtub full of fresh fish, wheelbarrows of flour, Venetian blinds hanging from the ceiling. My husband, artist Richard Kamler, has also provided huge bags of evocative objects at the top of shows for my improvisation partners and me to unpack. We've found cloven hoofs, sheets of Mylar, various foods, tools, face powder, pillows, ropes. Big fun.

In a recent performance, I was in a piece with Martin, playing someone who I felt was his aunt. The connection between us was strong and the piece felt real. It was one of those moments in the scene when we had arrived at a natural pause, between beats. I was clear that the piece was not complete, but had no impulse as to where to go next. These kind of moments can be scary. Or they can feel like exciting opportunities. Or both. When I looked at Martin I interpreted his silence and relative stillness to mean the ball was in my court. I felt a stab of anxiety. As this was happening I walked slowly backward (pure physical impulse) and found my hand resting on the soldier's jacket, from the army surplus store, that we'd placed on the back of a chair. I felt the heavy material under my hand, looked down, and immediately knew my next move. I picked up the jacket, approached Martin, and helped him put it on. As he fastened the three buttons, I saw that he was slumping, his chest caved in.

I said, "Stand up straight. Stick your chest out. You need to fill out that uniform." Martin adjusted his posture in a sad and comic way and proceeded to say his goodbyes to me as he was going reluctantly off (to war?). The jacket had been an evocative content trigger, a great help at that moment.

To prepare actors for using props, try these exercises:

REAL OBJECT TRANSFORMATION

Standing in a circle with the basket of props in the center, pick out an object. Players, one at a time, explore the possibilities of what this object might be used for: i.e., a hairbrush could be a telephone, a microphone, a tail or a penis. Pass the thing around the circle until many possibilities have been discovered. Then choose a new object. Try passing props again, this time use only one or two objects and have each actor endow the object with meaning by the way they handle the prop. Actors may also say a few words about it, i.e., "My grandmother gave me this scarf..."

ADD PROPS TO ENSEMBLE MOVEMENT

When the group is in the midst of any ensemble movement form, take enough props to equal half the number of movers and pass them out randomly. Ask players to explore integrating the props into their movement, giving and receiving the objects in a variety of ways, with one another.

TASKS, ADVANCED

In a piece, see what happens when students explore tasks with endowed objects, such as building or organizing something, or trying on clothes. How is the use of the body affected by the objects? How are players' moods affected? This requires multi-dimensional concentration for the players to remain fully available to their partners and to the progress of the piece. Try this with active movement and very sparse language.

30-SECOND CHAIR RULE

You may want use a chair, a bench or 2 or 3 wooden cubes onstage to create a very minimal set. If you have access to other furniture it's fruitful to explore ways to use it. When players sit on any piece of furniture I suggest that they get up within 30 seconds to avoid a static stage picture and the possibility of a "talking heads" scene. Also, remind them to use the bench or chair in ways other than sitting on it. And, in keeping with the principle of honoring what the piece needs, or in the case of an actor needing to sit, forget the chair rule.

COSTUME / CHARACTER EXPLORATION

Have students try on clothes from your basket and move in them. How does it affect their movement? How does the costume affect them emotionally? Does the image and feel of a character come up? It's helpful if you have a full-length mirror in the studio.

> *Love the art in yourself and not yourself in the art.*
>
> —*Constantin Stanislavski*

STRUCTURES FOR SCENES

TECHNIQUES FOR DUETS AND TRIOS

Ways to begin a scene:

- Two or three enter close together doing Reflect, Extend, Respond.

- All enter from opposite sides of stage with active movement and sound.

- First player enters and non-verbally establishes atmosphere and sense of place. Number two enters and offers first verbal life in response to what she sees in partner and feels in atmosphere.

- All enter in "Silent Tension" mode.

- Agree that one actor only will enter with an objective. (Other actors objectives will emerge in response.)

- An environment created by an artist, not seen before by players, is onstage and used as triggers for material.

- First player enters with props or furniture and clear attitude about the objects.

- The musician plays to establish mood before actors enter.

- One player comes in singing or laughing.

- All or only one or two enter with "Mantras."

- Actors come in with an image and feel of the animal that they are at that moment.

- Each player, without telling her partner, comes in with a pre-determined "where." Neither reality is named during the scene.

- Begin with a given movement quality (from audience) for each, or only one, player.

- Begin with given props (from audience) that must be used. (Place on chair or bench.)

- Begin with a given first line (from audience) that must be uttered.

Within a scene:

- One character is pre-occupied or has a secret or an uncommunicated message.

- One can't speak or can only speak one-, two- or three-word replies.

- Players incorporate gestures discovered earlier in Gesture Circle.

TRIOS

All the structures above, plus…

- Two on stage, third enters later.
- Number one enters in character she's developed (no given circumstances in mind); number two and number three enter open and receptive.
- All onstage at once in triangular composition.
- Two of the characters know each other well; the third only knows one of them.

IN-CLASS DISCUSSION RE TRIOS

Robert: I tend to feel intimidated by three-person scenes. They're so much harder than duets.

Joya: Well, let's think about that: the idea that they're difficult. Just holding that idea, believing it, can, of course, make the work more difficult. You could think: "Oh, I can do less in this scene, I can relax. I don't have to take so much responsibility."

Robert: I never thought of it that way.

Joya: So, what is it about trios that scares you?

Robert: You have to create relationships with two other people, not just one. And, I sometimes don't know what to do when the other two are relating and I don't see how I fit in.

Joya: Yes, you create relationships with everyone in your scene, so you need to sense for what your connection is to each character. How do you feel about him? What do you want? Of course, you may interact with one character more than the other, feel more connected to one. One player may have a more background part in the piece. That's all fine. The thing is to keep open and available to all players and see what happens. Just respond.

Everyone's trying to be really responsible and do their part and actually you can do much less. There could be silence or stillness or you could be purely in physical life, endowed with feeling, of course. You have more to respond to it, but it's easier because you don't have to carry it like you do in solo or duet. You don't always have to be in the limelight. Maybe you feel like an outsider?

Robert: Yeah, I often do.

Joya: Well, play that, the outsider, observing the others with a particular attitude. That's an interesting character. Use what's actually happening. Just live on stage. Something's always going on within you. Reveal that. You don't have to be making active offers all the time. Your particular presence is an offer. And, of course, you can use direct address, talking to the audience. Three is the perfect opportunity for that. When those two are doing something over there, you can come and talk to the audience. And if there's not a story happening among the three, well then you can find one for the audience in increments of direct address. And this might be a good time to work with props or the chair or a space object, which could help you create your own little world that is visually interesting.

In the trio structure of two starting onstage and the third entering later, I can see that most of you are waiting offstage until you know just what you'll do when you enter. What if you don't do that? What if you enter when you just feel drawn into the world onstage? Enter with a strong physical offer, and let your partners respond to you. Let them integrate you into the scene. You don't need to come in with a line that indicates endowment: "Hi Mom," or "Hi sexy," or "Can I borrow your lawn mower?" (all pretty cliché lines, yes?)—because it may be that when you get there, your fellow actors see you as something else. And since they've already established the world of the scene, it makes sense for them to have that opportunity. If they don't endow you in a little while, you can define yourself, if you feel you need to. Of course, we always welcome the emotionally more juicy choice.

When the third player is standing out of the scene "offstage" (though the audience can see you), if you're worrying about

"What am I going to say or do?" you're going to be in the analytical mind rather than in the instinctive self. Bring your physical and emotional life in and you'll find the next beat together with your partners.

WHAT ABOUT SCENES WITH FOUR, FIVE, OR MORE PLAYERS?

To be honest, I think it's really challenging to create a substantial and artful improvised theatre piece with more than five people on stage at once (even with more than three) unless the piece is movement-based (as in The Swamp, exercise on page 100). I've seen numerous troupes do it, relying on dialogue, and the results are often chaotic and muddy. The writing suffers. Of course, it can be done artfully if you are determined to do it. Actors will need to listen extra attentively and be especially aware of composition. They must be careful not to compete for the spotlight. If actors have learned to live onstage without speaking and are able to pass the focus around (and leave egos outside) this can work well.

Here are questions to address:

- Who is background and who is foreground (physical, visual composition) at any one moment?
- Who are the principal players and who are in the supporting roles?
- And, as always, what does the piece need?

If you think of background players as a chorus, they can echo lines of text or movement of primary players. They can sing or chant or play music. Also, larger groups can create rituals. See Ritual in the next chapter. The following exercise will help.

SPOTLIGHT
Advanced, 5 or more players

Performers begin a piece and use any of the structures above. The director has an imaginary spotlight that can move about as a follow spot. When all are onstage, the director will call out at intervals: "Spotlight, Harry's group," "Spotlight on Rebecca," etc. When actors hear this they cede the focus to the named group or individual. Background actor's behavior can become purely gestural and subtle, or actors can continue "speaking" silently.

NONIE KIMPITAK

SAMPLE CLASSES

The precise role of the artist, then, is to illuminate the darkness, blaze roads through that vast forest, so that we will not, in all our doing, lose sight of its purpose, which is, after all, to make the world a more human dwelling place.

—*James Baldwin*

When it came time to write out sample classes, I found myself full of resistance. I just didn't want to do it. There are so many possible combinations of exercises and structures, some appropriate for some groups, some for others. I love the idea of teachers and directors experimenting with these possibilities, keeping in mind the population of each particular class. Nevertheless, several people whose opinion I highly value insist that sample classes are needed in a book like this.

The suggestions below are for classes with a general FSI focus, including fundamentals. For specialized classes focusing on solo, movement, voice, or acting and character, draw from exercises in those categories.

For all three levels I've listed more than enough exercises for ten hours of class time (with breaks). How many and which exercises you use will vary greatly from class to class, depending on the skill level, number of students, and what discoveries and questions emerge from each exercise. Remember to debrief after some exercises.

For all classes, particularly when you meet with the same students repeatedly, consider elements of ritual, as described in the final section of this chapter. I have not incorporated ritual (other than the Closing Circle) in the list of activities per sample classes, but I encourage you to find elements of ritual that work for you.

SAMPLE CLASS
Beginner Level

Class format can run 2.5 to 7 hours.

It's important that the environment in which we study and practice has a wooden floor, is spacious, clean and light, and that we are free to make noise. A dance studio, with no mirrors or mirrors you can cover, is ideal. In order to give each student sufficient attention, I prefer to have a minimum of six and a maximum of 16 students in class. And if class is focusing on solo, no more than 12.

When new students register, I remind them to wear clothes they can move in and to bring a bottle of water. For long workshops, when we take a lunch break, the class mostly eats together, as this helps students form community.

A couple of things to notice about the exercises that follow:

1. This Beginner exercise list doesn't include much scene work, as in early beginner classes we don't focus on performance, although some exercises have a performance form. As the group progresses, more performance technique is introduced. Usually by class #3 (or #2 in long workshops) we'll do Let Your Partner Change You. Acting exercises are introduced when the teacher feels it's time.

2. Exercises focusing on physical (sound is physical) and emotional life come first in class. Exercises focusing on verbal life come later.

When the group is gathered, sitting in a circle on mats on the floor (with chairs provided for those who need them), after welcoming all, we begin class with a meditation.

FOUR-MINUTE MEDITATION

Meditation is done sitting or lying down, focusing on the breath. This is a time to "arrive" in class, to relax and clear the mind in preparation for our work together. I suggest that while meditating, students observe their body and mind.

CHECK IN

Teacher asks all students to share this information:

- Name (assuming they are new students)
- Psychophysical condition of the moment. (How's the body? Are they relaxed, anxious, exhausted, excited, pre-occupied...?)
- What impulse, need, or desire got them to class.

Going around the circle, this takes less than one minute per student unless a discussion about our work, that engages all, is triggered. Teacher does check in, too.

GROUP WARM-UPS

We stand to begin warm-ups, which are done in a circle. The teacher is almost always doing this right along with the group. In all classes, after or within the group warm up, score in time for students to do a few minutes of their own warm-up focusing on the specific needs of their body.

- Start with body alignment and awareness images (see warm-up section in Tuning the Instrument). Feel the feet on the floor, etc...Let the breath drop down to the bowl of the pelvis. This leads us to the Singing Yawn and other vocal and movement preparations drawn from the warm-up exercises, such as Kicks and Hoots, Marionettes, Sound Ball, Image Ball...
- Usually, after briefly warming up on our feet we'll drop down to the mats to do stretching and enlivening, deep relaxation, and sensory awareness. To get back to standing, use Help Each Other Up or Up and Down Three Ways.

When the group is relaxed and ready to reveal themselves, try:

- Self-Intro Three Ways
- Handshakes and Introductions
- Authentic Movement, and/or Linked Movement

MICHAEL ASTRAUSKAS

Follow with any combination of these exercises:

- Movement / Sound Reflecting Circle
- Trust Falls
- Group Go
- Group Yes
- Rolphing
- Mirror (and any variations that appeal) with possible Vocal Mirror
- Leader/Follower into ensemble movement with changing partners and/or with Tell Me About Yourself and possible partner intro. And/or
- Eye Contact Journey into ensemble movement with changing partners (Insert The Observer/Spatial Awareness in the midst of any ensemble movement activity)
- Stupid Dance
- Connections
- Develop That
- Given Movement Qualities / Known Text

Then (not necessarily in this order), once physical life is well explored, we are ready to add verbal life. In long workshops, this phase often begins after a food break.

Do a verbal warm-up first with Two-or-Three-Words-Per-Person stories, in the circle.

- Yes, And
- Monologue Circle or Pass the Story
- Two As One Speeches (if vocal mirror was done earlier)
- Gibberish Translator (with gibberish practice first)
- One Moves, One Talks and variations such as Both Move, One Talks
- Empty Vessel
- 2 or 3 Claps Solos

- For introduction to scenes, do Space/Shape followed by Repetition

For each exercise where some students perform while others are audience, decide whether to debrief (described under "Debriefing" in Chapter Three) following each individual performance. It's productive to do this, but if time is limited, the class may sometimes find it more useful to just do more activities with less discussion; consult them about their preference.

Conclude with Check Out and Closing Circle (see Ritual, below).

SAMPLE CLASS
Intermediate Level

- Meditation
- Check In

You may ask students to share something about themselves that the group doesn't yet know: one secret per class. Sometimes, especially for intermediate and advanced ongoing students, I'll add a question: i.e., Are there any requests for what you'd like to focus on? What has you excited today? Tell us what's making you vulnerable today? Or share a childhood memory, or what animal would you be today, or what body of water? You can make up these questions keeping self-revelation and stimulating the imagination in mind.

Then:

WARM UPS

Refer to warm-ups for Beginner Class, plus:

- Lion's Roar
- Up and Down Three Ways
- Sound Massage, and other body and voice preparations

EXERCISES

- Gesture Circle

- Movement / Sound Stimulus / Response Circle
- Emotion Dance and Stupid Dance
- Reflect, Extend, Respond
- Keeping Going into ensemble movement with addition of Instant Dreams. (Insert The Observer/ Spatial Awareness in the midst of any ensemble movement activity.)
- West Side Story
- Directors and Nouns and Directors and Change
- Vocal Variety
- Move and Talk Continuously
- Circle Monologue
- One Talks, One Moves and variations
- Over-Accepting
- Develop That
- Bad Acting
- Status Exercises
- Acting Objectives
- Prop / Costume exploration
- Greetings with Given Relationships
- Solo Stories from picture prompt
- Intercut Stories

SCENES

Monitor the transition to dialogue and interrupt scenes, coaching students to do PHYSICAL AND EMOTIONAL LIFE FIRST, if verbal life deadens physical life, resulting in disembodied "talking heads."

- Move on Every New Beat
- Let Your Partner Change You (first with no language, then with) and/or Silent Tension
- Checking Out and Closing Circle

Advanced classes are designed for improvisers and actors (with varying levels of experience) who perform or are preparing to perform. Some classes have a particular focus for that day, such as voice or narrative or integration of physical life/verbal life or character or solo...

- Meditation
- Check In with Underlining or other material sharing

After the group has met for a while we might do Underlining, bringing in material to share. As with the Intermediate class, the teacher may ask students to share something about themselves that the group doesn't yet know and may ask questions: Are there any requests? What's concerning or inspiring you today? Themes or stories circulating in your mind? Teacher/director may ask for reports on how their work is going. Then proceed to warm up.

Refer to warm-ups for Beginner Class, plus:

- Stream-of-Consciousness Warm-Up
- Vocal slide, stretching the face, horse's lips and other voice preparations
- Singing group song
- Song Circle / Rhythm Jam
- Cutting Loose
- Gesture Circle with sound (notice and remember some gestures)
- Reflect, Extend, Respond into The Swamp with or without props
- Voice Ladder

ACTING AND CHARACTER EXERCISES

- Explore Super Objectives
- Emotional recall and sense memory
- Ensemble Character through Physical Life

TWO AND THREE (AND MORE) PERSON SCENES

NONI KIMPITAK

Start with:

- Gestures from Circle or Silent Tension or Mantras or Given Props or any other performance structures or adjustments for scenes.
- The Real Thing
- Intercut Stories, possibly with Breaking into Scenes

SOLO EXERCISES

Solos from any solo structure such as:

- Two-Minute Solo: Rant/Celebrate
- Solo from Picture Prompt
- Living Sculpture
- Character from Worst/Best Traits
- Conclude with Check out and Closing Circle

ABOUT DEBRIEFING IN ADVANCED WORKSHOPS

A lot of time in advanced training is spent performing and critiquing pieces and addressing the particular strengths and challenges of each student. Sometimes, however, improvisers need to just get up and perform over and over with very little time spent on critique. This also gives us a chance to practice transitions from piece to piece.

RITUAL

Ritual is the conscious act of recognizing a life change and doing something to honor and support the change through the presence of such elements as witnesses, ceremony and sacred intention.

—Angeles Arrien

By ritual I mean an activity that responds to our needs creatively and marks or celebrates significant experience in our life: a repeatable, devotional act created with focus on community, symmetry, harmony, beauty.

Within FSI performance pieces, bits of mock or actual religious ritual sometimes arise. These may contain commentary on religion or they may mark an event that is part of the scene, such as a wedding or some magical transformation into some otherworldly creature. Or there may be rituals about an unnamed phenomenon.

Toning is a vocal activity with a ritual, transcendent feeling.

After warming up and doing conscious breathing, actors are lying on mats or on the floor (or sitting in a chair if needed). We gently begin to create sustained vowel sounds by releasing a long tone, usually an ahh or oh or aum. The leader may want to start the toning. We explore different pitches as we sound. After rich, full sound is established, we begin to slowly rise from the floor and walk about the space continuing our toning. We activate all our body awareness and spatial awareness. Though eyes are in soft focus we'll be connecting with each other by radiating energy three dimensionally as we move. The room will be awash with harmonics and an atmosphere of unity. At the risk of sounding corny, I'll say that a feeling of transcendence often permeates the space. This is ritual.

Rituals (that become familiar to the actors) at the beginning and ending of FSI classes and performances are very welcome, as there is much surprise and unpredictability in between.

The meditation and check-in circle that begin class may have a ritual quality, as do some of the movement and voice work we do in FSI, when players notice patterns emerging in both individual and ensemble movement and sound and consciously choose to repeat those patterns.

CIRCLE CLOSING RITUAL

I like to end almost every class with the Circle Closing Ritual.

- Before the ritual you may want to do a "check-out," in which actors speak three words that describe how they feel. It is also often helpful, especially with ongoing students, to ask if there are questions that arose in class and/or to talk briefly about what they learned.

Instructions for the Ritual:

- Holding the hands of the people next to you, first feel a hand in each of your hands. Then, feel a wrist in each of your hands (take hold of your neighbors' wrists) then an elbow in each of your hands, then shoulders, back of the neck, back of the waist, knees, top of the head. The circle will expand and contract as peoples' point of contact changes. The order of the movements may vary. There are often many soft smiles while doing this. It's kind of cuddly.
- When the circle is back to holding hands: Breathing in, let the arms float up. Let them come down slowly, with a slow vowel sound. Repeat twice more, a different vowel and pitch each time. The group will be moving and sounding in unison. Harmonics will emerge.
- The final action is the ensemble applauding itself.

MICHAEL ASTRAUSKAS

Joya, Owen Walker and Mike Sommers, Wildcat Studio, Berkeley 2017

NO FINAL PRODUCT

Perhaps there is no final product, no finished piece...
We are all of us people in the making.
And tomorrow we will do better.
Maybe that's how the creative process gets born:
from a constant dissonance between
impulse and thoughtfulness, self-confidence and self-doubt.
You will continue working because the work is never done.

—*Joshua Cory Kamler (my son)*

At the end of it all, the truth is that the creative process itself has no end and that every art form is a self-perpetuating process of making. Forever.

To sum up: there is no summing up. Improvisational Theatre is art in time. Like a Buddhist sand painting, it's gone as soon as it's finished. Years ago, I watched a group of Tibetan Buddhist Monks create a sand painting on the marble floor of the De Young Museum in San Francisco. They knelt for hours on end painstakingly pouring thin lines of colored sand to create a gorgeous image of a mandala. They were at it for days. When the huge painting was done, the monk artists conducted a brief ritual and then opened the giant doors at either end of the cavernous room. There was a collective gasp in the audience as the wind swooped in and blew the sand across the floor, and out into Golden Gate Park.

This is what improvisation is. The temporality of this work both thrills me and fills me with a desperate sense of loss. Each piece is unique to its moment. And it's comforting to know that new pieces await discovery. It's process that we embrace, that we love. Because at the end of it all, we will begin again.

JOYA CORY is an actor, director, improviser and educator
in the SF Bay Area. She is the
founder of the experimental
theatre troupes: MOTION: The
Women's Performing Collective
and LUCKY DOG THEATRE.
Her work has been recognized
with grants from the California Arts Council and the San
Francisco Foundation. Theatre
pieces she wrote and directed
have won the San Francisco
Bay Guardian Best Theatre of
the Year and Best of SF Fringe
awards. In workshops from
county jail to theatre venues,
Joya has taught almost two
thousand participants, adults
and children, beginners to
seasoned performers. Drawing
on 45 years of practice, exploring principles and techniques
from physical theatre, dramatic & narrative Improvisation,
movement & dance, comedy
improv, method acting, creative play & drama therapy, Joya
has developed FULL SPEC-
TRUM IMPROVISATION.

For up to date information
about classes and workshops,
visit: www.joyacory.com